She gasped again when she found herself suddenly crushed against his chest.

She could feel the steady thud of his heart beneath her breasts and was overwhelmed by a sudden need to lay her head on his chest. The past horrible year had sapped her strength, and he felt so strong, so capable. She would have given anything to lean on him, but she couldn't take the risk of getting used to having him take care of her.

'Are you all right?' he asked as she pulled away, and she shuddered when she heard the grating note in his voice. It was obvious that he'd been equally affected by her nearness, and it was hard to behave as though nothing had happened.

'I'm fine,' she said primly, and with a deliberate lack of warmth.

'Good.'

He gave her a tight smile. Fran didn't say anything as she followed him across the field. There wasn't

Jennifer Taylor lives in the north-west of England with her husband Bill. She had been writing Mills & Boon® romances for some years, but when she discovered Medical Romances™, she was so captivated by these heart-warming stories that she set out to write them herself! When not writing, or doing research for her latest book, Jennifer's hobbies include reading, travel, walking her dog and retail therapy (shopping!). Jennifer claims all that bending and stretching to reach the shelves is the best exercise possible. She's always delighted to hear from readers, so do visit her at www.jennifer-taylor.com

Recent titles by the same author:

THE MIDWIFE'S NEW YEAR WISH
RAPID RESPONSE
SURGEON IN CRISIS
THE PREGNANT SURGEON

A SPECIAL KIND
OF CARING

BY
JENNIFER TAYLOR

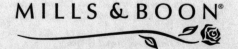

MILLS & BOON®

All the characters in this book have no existence outside the imagination of the author, and have no relation whatsoever to anyone bearing the same name or names. They are not even distantly inspired by any individual known or unknown to the author, and all the incidents are pure invention.

First published in Great Britain 2005
Harlequin Mills & Boon Limited,
Eton House, 18-24 Paradise Road, Richmond, Surrey TW9 1SR

© Jennifer Taylor 2005

ISBN 0 263 84318 1

Set in Times Roman 10½ on 11½ pt.
03-0705-56539

Printed and bound in Spain
by Litografía Rosés, S.A., Barcelona

CHAPTER ONE

'I WON'T lie to you and claim there's been a huge amount of interest in the post, Dr Goodwin. Few young doctors want to go into general practice these days, and fewer still want to work in the country. Teedale might be a beautiful place to live, but we're a long way from the bright city lights and you could find that working here rather restricts your social life.'

Alex Shepherd sat back in his chair and studied the young woman seated opposite him, hoping she couldn't tell that he was still in a state of shock. If he'd been surprised when he'd received her phone call that morning, requesting an interview, it was nothing to how he'd felt a few minutes ago when he'd seen her walking into the surgery.

Francesca Goodwin was stunningly beautiful: tall, slim, with thick auburn hair drawn back from her perfect oval face. Dressed in an elegant black trouser suit and high-heeled boots, she looked as though she'd stepped from the pages of one of those glossy women's magazines yet the CV she'd faxed through to him that day had proved that she had brains as well as beauty. If Alex had been asked to describe his ideal candidate for the post of junior partner at Teedale Surgery, he would never have come up with anyone as perfect as the gorgeous Dr Goodwin in a million years.

'I'm not interested in socialising, Dr Shepherd, so that really isn't a problem.'

Francesca Goodwin looked him squarely in the eyes and Alex felt a shiver run through him when he saw the chill in her deep grey eyes. Just for a moment he found himself wondering what had put it there before he dismissed the thought. If Dr Goodwin's interest in the job really was genuine then he couldn't afford to miss the chance of hiring her. The last twelve months had been a nightmare as he'd tried to juggle his work and look after Daniel. He knew that he'd been spending far too little time with his eight-year-old son but there simply weren't enough hours in a day to fit everything in. Taking on a partner was his only hope of putting some balance back into his life and he wasn't about to spoil his chances of achieving that. If life had been a little tough for Francesca Goodwin of late, it wasn't his concern.

Oddly enough that thought stuck in his craw and he cleared his throat. 'You could change your mind after you've lived here for a while. The pace of life in Teedale is very slow, although that doesn't mean we aren't extremely busy at the surgery. You might find that you spend more time at work than you do at home, in fact.'

'I'm not afraid of hard work, Dr Shepherd, as you can see from my references. As for the location of the town, well, that was one of its main attractions. I'm moving out of London because I want to live somewhere less hectic.'

'I see.'

Alex glanced at her CV although he could have recited it from memory by now. He must have read it at least a dozen times already but he needed a moment to digest what she'd said. Although she'd sounded sincere, he found it difficult to accept that a woman as beautiful and as talented as this would want to bury herself in the country. It seemed a little too good to be true, in fact, and he couldn't help wondering if there was a catch.

'Is there a problem, Dr Shepherd?'

The question made him look up and he frowned when he saw a spark of irritation light her eyes before she quickly blanked it out. It was obvious the beautiful Dr Goodwin didn't appreciate him having doubts about her and he found it intriguing that she didn't come out and say so. There was something about her which told him that she didn't normally mince her words, yet she was keeping a tight rein on herself that day. Was she so anxious to get this job that she was afraid to say anything that might ruin her chances?

'Not that I'm aware of.'

Alex gave himself a mental shake when he realised that he was in danger of getting sidetracked again. So long as he was sure that she was suitably qualified for the post, that should be all that mattered. He glanced at her CV again, pinpointing the one fact that had bothered him from the beginning.

'Your references are excellent, Dr Goodwin, and you've obviously gained a great deal of experience in the three years since you qualified. The only thing I find somewhat surprising is that you left your last post before you'd found another position. Is there a reason why you decided to leave before securing another post?'

'My reasons for leaving were personal and had no bearing on my ability to do the job.' Francesca Goodwin's tone was icy now. 'If you wish to verify that then I'm sure Dr Walters will confirm that he was happy with my work.'

'I'm sure he was and I apologise if you thought I was implying anything untoward had happened,' he said quietly, feeling suitably rebuked.

He sighed, wondering if it might be safer to leave it at that. It would be easy enough to confirm what she'd told him so there was no point making an issue of it, was there? Obviously, Francesca's decision to leave her last job was a rather thorny subject and although he was curious to know what had happened, he didn't want it to become a sticking point. If there was a chance that he could make Daniel's life a bit more normal then he was going to offer her the job and be done with it.

His heart gave a little hiccup at the thought of them working together but he battened it down. He wasn't going to start creating problems by heading down *that* route. He smiled at her, hoping to warm up the rather chilly atmosphere that had descended upon them.

'I'm not sure if you know that the job comes with accommodation as part of the package. There was a bit of a mix-up with some of the ads and a couple of them didn't include that fact. Anyway, it's nothing special—just a small cottage next to the surgery but it will save you having to find somewhere to live if you do decide to move here.'

'I did know about the cottage. It was another reason why I thought this post would suit me.'

She stared back at him, her beautiful face betraying so little emotion that his heart performed another of those little flip-flops. Crazy though it sounded, he'd have given anything to see her smile.

'Oh, right. That's great. Daniel will be thrilled when I tell him because it was his idea to advertise the cottage along with the job.' Alex knew he was gabbling but it seemed safer to occupy his mind rather than allow it to keep racing off at tangents all the time. 'He insisted it would be a good selling point and he was obviously right.'

'Indeed,' Francesca replied politely although he was very conscious that she didn't ask him any questions—and that was another little puzzle, of course.

Most people when presented with a nugget of information like that would have asked who Daniel was, but she didn't appear to be interested. The only thing that seemed to interest her was the job so he decided that he'd be better off sticking to that. He pushed back his chair and stood up.

'In that case, would you like to see the cottage? You'd probably feel happier if you had some idea what you might be letting yourself in for.'

'I'm sure it will be perfectly adequate for my needs,' she said coolly, making no attempt to rise.

'I hope so, but I'd prefer it if you would take a look just to check.'

Alex couldn't explain it but for some reason it seemed important that she should see the cottage rather than rely on his say-so that it would be suitable for her. After all, who in her right mind would agree to move into a place without first checking it out? he wondered, taking the key out of his desk drawer. He certainly wouldn't and he couldn't understand why Francesca would be prepared to do so either.

He took his coat off the back of his chair, wondering why she gave out such mixed signals. On the one hand she exuded confidence and on the other she seemed oddly unsure, almost scared. Despite his resolve to stick strictly to the issue of the job, he realised that he wanted to find out more about her. Maybe he could get her talking once they left the surgery?

It was a tantalising thought so he hastily shrugged on his jacket. 'Shall we take a look at the place then?'

'If you insist.' Francesca stood up, the very stiffness of her posture as she led the way from the room telling him that she thought it was a waste of time.

Maybe it was, he conceded as he followed her along the corridor, but now that he'd got this far, he wasn't going to back down. They reached the waiting room and he stopped to tell his receptionist where they were going. Although afternoon surgery wasn't due to start for another half-hour there were several people waiting to see him and he sighed when he saw the curious glances being cast their way as he followed Francesca outside.

The village gossips would have a field day if he hired her. It had been four years since Trish, his wife, had died and everyone in Teedale seemed to believe it was high time he got married again. Maybe he should warn Francesca what she could be letting herself in for, but how exactly should he set about it? Perhaps a quiet word in her ear along the lines of *Oh, by the way, you do know that the villagers are longing to marry me off and that you'll be fair game if you take the job* would do the trick?

He groaned because he could just imagine the lovely Francesca's response if he told her that. She'd probably high-tail it out of Teedale and that would be the last he'd see of her!

Francesca felt a spasm run through her when she heard Alex Shepherd groan. She didn't glance round, however, but carried on walking down the path, wishing with all her heart that the interview was over. Although Dr Shepherd had been nothing less than courteous, there was something about him that warned her it would be a mistake to lie to him. Just for a moment she found herself wondering if she should have told him the truth about her reasons for leaving London before she briskly dismissed the idea. What had happened in her private life was none of his business.

'Here we are.'

He touched her lightly on the arm and Fran stopped. She moved aside while he unlocked the cottage door, not wanting to give him a reason to touch her again. The lock was stiff and she heard him grunt as he struggled to turn the key but she didn't say anything. He might have insisted that she must see the cottage but she didn't intend to let this turn into a discussion about the pros and cons of her living there. What Alex Shepherd didn't know was that she didn't have a choice.

Her flat in London had been sold weeks ago and she'd been renting a room there ever since. Even though the place was tiny, the rent was exorbitant. Although her solicitor had told her there would be some money left once all the bills were paid, it would be weeks before she could get hold of it. She had just enough cash to last her until the end of the month then she'd be in real trouble. Basically, it was this cottage or nothing and for a second panic rose inside her as she tried to imagine what she would do if she didn't get the job, before she ruthlessly stamped it out. She couldn't afford to let Alex Shepherd know how desperate she was or he would start asking questions.

He finally managed to get the door open and turned to her. 'Sorry about that. The lock needs oiling but I'll get it sorted before you move in. Now, I think you'd better let me go first.'

He grinned at her, his hazel eyes so full of warmth that despite herself Fran found herself responding. 'I'm not trying to come over all macho, you understand, but the place has been shut up for months so there could be the odd bit of wildlife lurking about. I'd hate you to come face to face with something small and furry!'

'I'm not afraid of mice,' she stated coldly because she hated the fact that she could still respond to a man's smile after what had happened. She strode past him, trying to ignore the pain that lanced her heart. She wasn't going to think about *Paul's* smile and how it had made her feel. That was all in the past and she had to concentrate on the future now, and the future meant this cottage and a job in a small Derbyshire village, miles away from everyone she knew.

It would be a relief to get away but she couldn't pretend that she didn't feel a bit panicky when she thought about the changes she would need to make to her life if she moved to Teedale. She'd always lived in the city so would she be able to adapt to such a different way of life? What if she hated living here or, worse still, couldn't handle the work that was expected of a country GP?

She couldn't see herself going back to London and facing everyone again. It had been bad enough these last few months. Her friends had been very sympathetic but she didn't want their pity. She wanted to get on with her life and if that meant moving to the country, that was what she would do. The thought steadied her so that she was able to look calmly at Alex Shepherd when he laughed.

'You're obviously braver than me because I hate the little beggars and I don't mind admitting it. If I had my way our house would be declared a mouse-free zone but Daniel won't hear of me setting traps for them.'

He pocketed the key then closed the door, effectively shutting out the daylight. Fran didn't say anything as she waited for him to switch on the lights even though she knew what was expected of her. He probably expected her to ask about Daniel but she wasn't going to.

The truth was that she didn't want to know about Alex Shepherd's life outside work because she didn't intend to tell him anything about her own. Her life had been picked over until she felt ill just thinking about all the gossip and now she wanted some privacy. The sooner he understood that she only wanted a job from him, not friendship, the easier it would be for both of them, yet it was strangely difficult to ignore him. Despite his easygoing manner, he wasn't a man one could easily disregard, she realised with a sinking heart.

'Damn! The bulb must have gone.' Alex tried flicking the light switch on and off a couple more times then sighed. 'No joy, I'm afraid. Hang on a sec while I find a torch. I'm almost sure there's one in the kitchen.'

Fran didn't have time to move out of the way this time before he brushed past her. She took a deep breath but that accidental touch of a masculine hand in the darkness had unleashed a flood of memories: fingertips caressing her skin; breath warming her cheek; the reassurance of a strong male body lying beside her in the night...

'Got it!'

She bit her lip when Alex came back with the torch, praying that he wouldn't notice she was upset because the last thing she needed was him trying to comfort her. She had to stand on her own two feet and couldn't afford to make the mistake of relying on someone else ever again.

'So what do you think?'

Mercifully, he seemed oblivious to her dilemma as he swept the beam of the torch around the room. Fran breathed out a sigh of relief when she realised that she'd got away with it this time. She wouldn't allow herself to get so emotional again, she promised herself as she looked around. However, she couldn't deny that her spirits plummeted when she saw the state of the place. It was one thing to tell herself that she didn't mind where she lived, but it was another thing entirely to be presented with the grim reality. As her gaze skimmed over the cobwebs and grime, she was hard-pressed not to burst into tears. The place was a dump and she couldn't imagine living here, but what choice did she have?

'You hate it, don't you?' Alex Shepherd's voice was filled with contrition as he panned the beam of the torch around the room once more. 'No wonder. I should have had the place cleaned up before I showed you around.'

'No, it's fine,' she said quickly because she hated to hear him sounding so upset. A spasm shot through her because worrying about his feelings shouldn't have been an issue.

'Oh, come on. There's being polite and there's being *polite*! The place is a tip and I need shooting for suggesting that you might want to live here.' He angled the torch so that it lit up the cobweb-encrusted ceiling. 'It's not even habitable.'

'It just needs a good clean and a coat of paint.' She saw the sceptical look he shot her and shrugged. 'It will look miles better once all those cobwebs have been cleared away.'

'Your middle name doesn't happen to be Pollyanna, does it?' He grinned when she looked at him in confusion. 'Only a born optimist could find anything good to say about the place. No, I won't hear of you staying here, Francesca. I'll find somewhere else for you to stay—maybe the B&B down the road. It does a roaring trade in the summer although business drops off at this time of the year—'

'I can't afford to stay in a B&B.'

The admission rushed out before she could think better of it and she saw him frown. She held her breath because he was bound to ask her why she couldn't afford to stay in a B&B. After all, she'd earned a decent enough salary since she'd qualified and it was only natural that he would expect her to have some money put aside so how was she going to explain that she had only a few pounds to her name?

She could tell him the truth, of course, that Paul had taken all her savings as well as her self-respect. She could also tell him that she'd even remortgaged her flat and invested every penny she'd raised in Paul's business then lost that as well when the firm had gone bust. The problem was that he'd wonder what sort of a fool she was if she told him that, and if he really wanted someone as stupid as her working in his practice…

'Alex, are you there? Alex!'

Fran jumped when someone banged on the cottage door. She moved aside as Alex went to open it but her heart was pounding when she realised what a difficult position she was in. She didn't *want* to lie to him but telling him the truth might very well scupper her chances of getting this job. It was little wonder that she found it difficult to remain calm as she watched his receptionist rush into the cottage.

'Oh, thank heavens you're still here!' the woman exclaimed. 'I wasn't sure if you'd decided to show Dr Goodwin around the village as well.'

'We haven't had time to look round the cottage properly yet, Mary,' Alex pointed out dryly. 'So what's the panic? Has someone turned up without an appointment?'

'No, no, nothing like that. Daniel's teacher just phoned

to say that he's had an accident. Apparently, he fell off the climbing frame during PE. Mrs Monroe said to tell you that she's phoned for an ambulance—'

'How long ago did it happen?' Alex cut in. Fran could hear the fear in his voice and, despite her resolve to remain impartial, felt her own heartbeat quicken in alarm.

'About ten minutes ago,' Mary explained. 'I came straight to find you as soon as I'd finished speaking to Mrs Monroe.'

'That means the ambulance won't have arrived at the school yet.'

He didn't waste any more time as he ran out of the cottage. Mary hurried after him and after a moment's hesitation Fran locked the cottage and followed them. Alex was way ahead of her by then and she saw him make straight to a rather battered-looking Land Rover that was parked in front of the surgery. He opened the door then paused when Mary grabbed hold of his arm.

'But what about the patients, Alex? There's at least a dozen people waiting to see you so what should I tell them?'

He gently removed the receptionist's hand and slid behind the wheel. He started the engine then glanced over to where Fran was standing.

'Do you still want the job?'

'I…um… Yes, of course I do,' she said hurriedly.

'Then it's yours.' He turned to Mary again. 'I'll leave Dr Goodwin in your capable hands. Show her where everything is kept, will you? I'll be back as soon as I can but I might not make it before surgery ends.'

With that, he backed out of the parking space. Fran's mouth dropped open as she watched him driving away. She'd never imagined when she'd set out for the interview that she'd end up taking surgery but, obviously, that was what he expected her to do.

Just for a moment panic rose inside her before she both mentally and physically squared her shoulders. She'd done what she'd set out to do and had got herself a job in the country so now it was up to her to make it work!

CHAPTER TWO

'IF YOU could just raise your arms for me, Mrs Price… that's fine.'

Fran ran her fingers over the woman's right breast and nodded. 'Yes, I see what you mean. When did you first notice that you had lumps in your breasts?'

'Yesterday morning when I was having a shower. I spotted them when I was shaving under my arms,' Kathleen Price explained.

Kathleen was an attractive woman in her forties with dark hair and a friendly manner. She'd seemed relieved when she'd come into the consulting room and Fran had introduced herself. Although none of the patients had cancelled their appointments, Fran had sensed that a few people had been uneasy about seeing a stranger. Obviously, Kathleen Price didn't share their concerns, however, and Fran smiled warmly at her.

'Then award yourself some extra brownie points for having the good sense to get them checked out so promptly.'

'I very nearly didn't!' Kathleen admitted, laughing. 'I know it must sound daft to you, Dr Goodwin, but I get ever so embarrassed if I have to discuss something like this with Alex. Oh, don't get me wrong—he's really lovely to talk to but I feel so self-conscious about having to strip off in front of a man.' Kathleen rolled her eyes. 'And me a farmer's wife with three grown-up sons, too. You'd have thought I'd have got over all that nonsense years ago.'

'A lot of women feel exactly the same as you do,' Fran assured her. 'That's why it's so useful to have a female doctor in the practice.'

17

'Oh, it is. I'm so pleased that you're going to be working here and I know a lot of women in the village will feel the same. We've really missed having a woman doctor to discuss our problems with since Trish died.'

'Trish? She was Dr Shepherd's partner, I assume?' Fran asked, carefully examining the woman's left breast. There was a slight lumpiness in the upper, outer part of the breast but it wasn't nearly so noticeable as the swellings in the right breast.

'Not just his partner, I'm afraid. Trish was also his wife.' Kathleen sighed when Fran looked at her in surprise. 'They made such a lovely couple, too, and obviously thought the world of each other. Little Daniel was just four when Trish was killed and it hit him really hard. He was in the car, you see, when the tanker ran into them and killed her, although there wasn't a scratch on him when they got him out. Mary told me the poor little mite kept having nightmares for months afterwards. I don't know how Alex coped with it all.'

'It must have been a very difficult time for him,' Fran said tonelessly because she didn't want to encourage Kathleen to tell her anything else. Maybe it was cowardly but she didn't want to think about the heartache Alex must have suffered, dealing with his own grief over his wife's death as well as his child's distress. Something warned her that she would find it too difficult to remain detached if she allowed herself to dwell on it.

'You can get dressed now, Mrs Price,' she said, deliberately changing the subject. 'I've seen everything I need to for now.'

'So do you know what's wrong with me then, Doctor?'

Kathleen Price popped her bra back on and Fran was relieved to see that she'd successfully managed to distract her from the subject of Alex Shepherd's family life.

'I'm almost certain that you're suffering from fibroadenosis.' Fran sat down behind the desk, feeling easier now they were back on safe ground. 'It's fairly common in women in your age group and basically just means that you've developed cysts, or fluid-filled tissue sacs, in your breasts.'

'So it's not cancerous, then?' Kathleen asked her, putting her coat back on. 'Obviously, that was my main worry, you understand. You read all those articles, telling you to check your breasts for lumps, so you immediately start imagining the worst when you find something wrong.'

'Of course you do, but there's really no need to worry unduly, Mrs Price,' Fran assured her. 'Fibroadenosis isn't an indication that there are cancer cells present. It's caused by an overgrowth of glandular and fibrous tissue which causes the lumps and cysts to form inside the breasts. Another name for it is chronic mastitis.'

'Mastitis?' Kathleen laughed out loud. 'Oh, wait till I tell my husband that! We run a dairy farm and it isn't unknown for one of our cows to get mastitis from time to time.'

Fran laughed. 'I think you could be in line for some teasing.'

'I certainly will if my boys find out,' Kathleen agreed ruefully. 'Do you have any children, Dr Goodwin? If so then I'm sure you'll understand why I'd prefer to keep this from them.'

'No, I don't have any children but I can imagine the fun yours would have,' she said quietly, trying to ignore the pang her heart gave because if everything had gone to plan, she might have been pregnant by now.

She picked up her pen, not wanting Kathleen to see that she was upset. She'd always wanted a family although Paul had never been as keen on the idea. He'd refused to discuss it whenever she'd tried to raise the subject, although it had been Paul who'd suggested they should try for a baby last Christmas. At the time, Fran had been so thrilled that she'd never questioned why he'd had a change of heart. Of course, they'd seemed so happy that there'd been no reason to suspect that he'd had an ulterior motive. It was only later that she'd realised the truth, when all the other lies had started to surface.

Paul had told her that the only way they could afford a baby was if she remortgaged her flat and invested the money in his business. His firm had been going through a bad patch, he'd explained, and he wanted to be sure they were financially secure if they were going to start a family.

Fran had agreed immediately, as he'd known she would, and it was hard to deal with the thought of how stupid she'd been. Paul had used the promise of a baby to get what he'd wanted and she'd fallen for the ruse the same as she'd fallen for the rest of his trickery. It made her feel sick to recall how he'd used her, so it was a relief to focus on Kathleen's problems rather than the mess she'd made of her life.

'Whilst I'm ninety per cent certain that my diagnosis is correct, I'd feel happier if we covered every angle.' She took a pad out of the drawer and jotted down Kathleen's name. 'I'm going to put in a request for you to have a mammogram. It's very straightforward and the procedure will be explained to you at the time so there's no need to worry about it. Unfortunately, I'm not sure what the system is in this area so I can't tell you how long it will be before you get an appointment. I'll need to check with Dr Shepherd, but hopefully it shouldn't be more than a week or so before you're seen.'

'That's fine by me, Doctor. I just feel so much better now that I know you don't think I've got something horrible growing inside me.'

'I'm sure you do,' she agreed sympathetically. 'As for the lumps, you'll probably find them worse just before you have a period. I expect your breasts have been feeling rather tender and swollen recently but it's nothing to worry about.

There's no specific treatment but if the symptoms become too uncomfortable I can prescribe diuretics to get rid of the fluid and if they don't work then there are a few other drugs we can try. However, a lot of women find that a warm flannel laid over the breast helps to ease the discomfort better than anything else does.'

'Just like we do with our cows.' Kathleen laughed as she offered Fran her hand. 'I think I'll just have to grin and bear it otherwise my life will be hell. Anyway, thank you again, Dr Goodwin. I really appreciate your kindness. And if I didn't say it before then I'll say it now. Welcome to Teedale! I hope you'll be very happy with us.'

'Thank you,' Fran said huskily, deeply touched.

She saw Kathleen out then sat down and thought about what had happened. For months now she'd felt like a pariah yet there was no doubt that Kathleen had been genuinely pleased about her working there. It made her see that she'd been right to decide to move out of London and make a fresh start. It wouldn't be easy to rebuild her life but she'd manage it. Somehow.

Her spirits suddenly lifted because for the first time in ages she had something to look forward to. This job could turn out to be her salvation so long as she stuck to her self-imposed rules and kept well away from Alex Shepherd outside working hours. Maybe it was silly to be so wary, but there was something about him which warned her it would be a mistake to get involved in his affairs. She'd had her heart broken once and she wasn't going to put herself in the position of having it broken a second time.

Alex parked the car in front of the surgery and switched off the engine although he made no attempt to get out. The mind-numbing fear he'd experienced on hearing that Daniel had been injured had left him feeling so drained that he wasn't sure if his legs would support him.

He let his head fall forward onto the steering-wheel and practised some of the deep-breathing techniques he often advocated for his patients, but his nerves were still jangling and would continue to do so until he was allowed to bring his son home.

The paediatrician had decided to keep Daniel in hospital overnight as a precaution because he'd banged his head and whilst Alex agreed with the decision, it didn't make it any easier to bear. He would have given anything to bring his son home but he had to be sensible and not start acting like an over-anxious parent. Daniel would be fine in the hospital so now he would have to see what sort of havoc the beautiful Dr Goodwin had created in his surgery.

Alex sighed as he forced himself to get out of the car. He really and truly didn't feel like dealing with anything else that night but he had a duty to his patients as well as to his newest member of staff. It had been a bit rich to go rushing off like that so he could hardly complain if Francesca had made a pig's ear of everything. Friday was their busiest night because they didn't open on Saturday so there'd probably been a queue of people a mile long waiting to be seen. Although he didn't doubt that Francesca would have done her best, coping in a strange surgery and with patients who could be a bit prickly if you didn't know them wouldn't have been easy and he felt a rush of guilt assail him as he opened the surgery door. He'd had no right to drop her in at the deep end like that.

'Oh, so there you are, Alex. How's Daniel?'

'He's fine. They're keeping him overnight because he banged his head but he should be allowed home in the morning,' Alex replied, somewhat surprised by the cheerfulness of Mary's greeting. Fond though he was of his receptionist, she did tend to panic in a crisis and he'd assumed that she would be in a pretty bad state by the time he arrived. However, there was no sign of panic on her face and no sign of the pandemonium he'd been expecting either. As he looked around the almost empty waiting room, Alex found it impossible to hide his surprise and he heard Mary laugh.

'It's wonderful, isn't it? Dr Goodwin has zipped through the list at a rate of knots. Oh, there was the odd moan, of course—you know what some of the patients can be like when they have to see someone new—but even they came out singing her praises.' Mary wagged an admonishing finger at him. 'You'll have to look to your laurels if you hope to keep up with her.'

'So it appears,' he agreed in bemusement. He glanced round when old Tom Carter, one of their surliest and most difficult patients, came shuffling along the corridor on his way back from the consulting room.

'Everything all right, Tom?' he asked, waiting for the usual litany of moans, but, amazingly, Tom sounded positively happy for once.

'Aye, fine, thank you, Dr Shepherd. That's a nice young lady you've hired to work here, I must say. Has a lovely way with her, she has. Reminds me a lot of my Ethel, she does. They're much alike.'

'Oh, um, right. That's great,' Alex floundered, desperately trying to find some similarity between Tom's elderly, arthritic wife and the gorgeous Dr Goodwin. He failed—miserably—so turned to Mary after Tom had bade them a cheery goodnight.

'I'll just have a quick word with Dr Goodwin before you send in the next patient. She can bring me up to speed.'

'No problem. We seem to be ahead of schedule for once so we've plenty of time,' Mary assured him, happily checking the appointment book.

Alex forbore to say anything as he made his way along the corridor but it was slightly galling to realise how well Francesca had managed in his absence. As he knocked on the door, he found himself wondering once again why a woman so eminently capable as her would choose to work in a small country practice. Was she running away from something? Or from some*one*, perhaps?

'Come in… Oh, it's you.'

Alex tried to hide his disgruntlement when Francesca's welcoming smile faded the moment she realised it had been him knocking on the door and not a patient. 'No need to ask how you've managed,' he said with an attempt at joviality which didn't quite ring true. 'I expected to find a queue of patients out there but the waiting room is almost empty and Mary is singing your praises.'

'The list wasn't any longer than what I've been used to dealing with,' she replied coolly, lining up the patients' notes so that they formed a perfect tower on the corner of the desk.

'Obviously not. However, it isn't easy to step in at a moment's notice and I admire the way you've handled things so efficiently.'

Alex couldn't explain it but it stung to hear her speak to him in such a frosty manner when she'd obviously treated his patients very differently. He went over to the desk and took the top file off the pile. 'Old Tom Carter can be a bit gruff at times so I hope he didn't cause you too many problems.'

'Not at all. He was telling me about his childhood and how he and his brothers used to do all the haymaking on their father's farm in the summer.'

'Really?' Alex managed to smile but he couldn't remember having a conversation with Tom during the whole time he'd been running the practice. He dropped the old man's file onto the desk and picked up another, hoping Francesca couldn't tell that he felt rather put out about Tom's lack of allegiance. Kathleen Price's name leapt out at him and he frowned.

'We don't often see Kathleen in the surgery. What was wrong with her tonight?'

'Fibroadenosis. I'll refer her for a mammogram, of course, but I'm fairly confident it's nothing more serious than that.'

'She'll need to go to Derby for the mammogram. We do have a mobile screening unit which visits Teedale each year but it isn't due here until the summer,' he explained as he read through the notes Francesca had written. 'I'll get it sorted out then ask Kathleen to pop in so I can explain everything to her. She's not had a mammogram before so she might find it reassuring to have some idea about what will happen on the day.'

'Quite apart from the fact that I've already covered everything, Dr Shepherd, the patient might not feel too happy about discussing this issue with you. She mentioned that she prefers to see a female doctor about some problems and this happens to be one of them.' Francesca's tone was icily polite but that didn't disguise the reproof it held. 'If you could just tell me whom I should contact to arrange an appointment for Mrs Price, that will be sufficient.'

Alex sighed when he realised that he'd unwittingly stepped on her toes. 'Of course. I'll ask Mary to print out a list of contacts for you. We refer most of our patients to Derby but you'll soon get to know who everyone is. And I apologise if you thought I was interfering. I never meant to imply that you hadn't dealt with the case properly.'

He grimaced when she didn't say anything. 'It's a question of old habits dying hard, I'm afraid. I'm so used to being the sole provider of care for the people in this village that I just naturally assume responsibility. I'll have to stop doing that now you're here.'

'It would be extremely difficult to work together if you felt you had to question every decision I made.'

'It would, and I promise you that it won't happen again.'

He grinned as he made the sign of a cross on his chest. 'Cross my heart and hope to die?'

Her mouth twitched at such a childish bit of nonsense and Alex found he was holding his breath as he waited to see if she would relent enough to smile. He swallowed a sigh when in the end she simply looked away. He knew it was silly but he couldn't help feeling deflated at having his hopes dashed again.

'So was there anything else you needed to ask me?' he said quickly because it was ridiculous to start worrying because Francesca hadn't smiled at him.

'Not really… Oh, yes, a patient by the name of Peter Arkwright came in tonight.' She riffled through the folders until she found the one she wanted and handed it to him. 'As you can see from my notes, he was complaining of some rather vague symptoms—headaches, bouts of fever, shivering and sweats—that sort of thing. He told me that it had happened a couple of times in the past few months. I couldn't find anything obviously wrong when I examined him so I think he needs a blood test. I decided not to do it tonight because I wasn't sure when the samples would be collected.'

'Every weekday morning at eleven,' Alex explained promptly. 'We get everyone in first thing and take the samples so they're ready when the courier arrives. It takes a day or two for the results to be faxed through, but the lab we use is usually pretty efficient.'

'That's fine. I'll tell Mary to phone Mr Arkwright and ask him to pop in on Monday morning. Would eight o'clock be all right?'

'Fine. I'm usually here by then although I nip out for a few minutes to take Daniel to school.'

'You don't have a practice nurse to do the bloods?'

'Hilary comes in three afternoons a week to help with the clinics—antenatal, asthma, that type of thing,' he explained, very conscious that once again she'd avoided asking about Daniel. Bearing in mind the reason he'd had to go rushing off and leave her in the first place had been because of his son, he found it very strange. Didn't she like children? Or was there more to it than that?

'So basically it will be just you and me working in the surgery each day?'

'That's right.' He pushed the question to the back of his mind because he was too tired to deal with it at that moment. He dredged up a smile, wondering why he was so interested in the first place when it was patently obvious that she wasn't interested in him.

'This is quite a small practice compared to some of the big city ones you're used to, but geographically, we cover a very large area. A lot of our patients are farmers so you could find that you have to drive a fair distance to do any house calls.' He paused as a thought struck him. 'You can drive? I never thought to ask you that before.'

'Yes, so there's no need to worry,' she assured him and he sighed in relief.

'Phew! Thank heavens for that. It would be impossible to do this job without a car, I'm afraid.' He frowned. 'Now that I think about it, though, I don't remember seeing a car outside when I came in just now. Didn't you park in front of the surgery?'

'I didn't come by car today. I thought it would be easier if I came by train because I don't know the area. I took a taxi from the station in Beesley, which reminds me that I'll need to phone for one to take me back there. Do you have the number of a local taxi firm, by any chance?'

'You're travelling back to London tonight by train?' Alex couldn't hide his dismay and he saw Francesca look at him in surprise.

'Of course.' She glanced at her watch. 'What time do the London trains run at this time of the night? I've missed the one I was planning on getting so I'll have to catch the next one and just hope there's a seat left.'

'That could be a little difficult,' he murmured uncomfortably.

'Difficult? What do you mean by that?'

Her tone had sharpened but he'd seen the flash of alarm in her eyes and cursed himself for not thinking about what he'd been doing when he'd asked her to take surgery. His only concern at the time had been Daniel, of course, and he hadn't given any thought to the problems it would cause by asking Francesca to cover for him.

'I asked you a question, Dr Shepherd. Please will you be kind enough to answer it.'

There was a definite wobble in her voice now and Alex realised with a sinking heart that he couldn't prolong her agony. Even though it felt on a par with pulling the wings off a butterfly, he had to break the bad news to her.

'I'm afraid there aren't any more trains to London tonight. The last one left at six o'clock.'

'But it's ten minutes past six now!' She stared at him in dismay. 'You mean that I'll have to wait until the morning before I can leave here?'

'No, it's not that simple, I'm afraid.'

He gritted his teeth because there was no point trying to absolve himself by apologising. He'd completely messed up and ruined her plans. The least he could do now was to tell her the truth and hope that she would forgive him.

Eventually.

'The line is closed this weekend while the engineers carry out repairs to the track. The next train to London won't leave until Monday morning. I'm really sorry, Francesca, but it looks as though you're stuck here for the weekend.'

CHAPTER THREE

'THE weekend... But that's ridiculous! I can't possibly stay here for the whole weekend. I have things to do!'

'I don't see that you have much choice.'

Fran bit her lip when she heard the certainty in Alex's voice. She could feel a wave of panic rising inside her but she refused to let him see just how worried she was. 'I could hire a car and drive myself back to London,' she suggested as calmly as she could.

'The nearest car hire depot is in Derby and it will be shut by the time you get there,' he explained gently. 'I'd offer to lend you my car but I'll need it to fetch Daniel from the hospital in the morning. And of course if you drove it back to London, I'd be really stuck if I got called out. I don't use an on-call service because of the difficulty of finding some of the outlying farms.'

'But there must be a way to get back,' she protested, desperately trying to come up with a viable solution. 'I know—how about a coach? Do the London coaches run from Beesley?'

'Once again you'd have to go to Derby because that's the nearest pick-up point for the London coaches.' He shrugged. 'You'd have to get a taxi because there aren't any buses at this time of the night, and that's assuming you could find a driver willing to take you. The local firm only goes as far as Beesley, I'm afraid.'

'So what you're really saying is that I'm going to have to stay here whether I like it or not?' she said slowly, unable to hide her dismay any longer.

'I'm afraid so.' He sighed. 'Look, Francesca, if there was

any way I could get you back to London tonight, I'd do so. It's my fault that you're stuck here and I feel really guilty about it, too. I just can't see a way around the problem, can you?'

'Not from what you've told me,' she said shortly because there was no point going round in circles when it wouldn't achieve anything.

She took a deep breath, trying to remain calm, but she'd never envisaged something like this happening. 'I'm going to need a place to sleep if I have to stay here so can you suggest somewhere?'

'The B&B down the road,' he said promptly, obviously relieved that she'd accepted the inevitable.

Fran had to admit to a certain sympathy for him because it was obvious how guilty he felt. However, the last thing she needed was to start worrying about his feelings if she was going to spend the weekend in Teedale, so she ruthlessly stamped it out.

'Why don't I give them a call and book you in?' He picked up the phone and smiled encouragingly at her. 'They're bound to have a vacancy at this time of the year and you'll be very comfortable there.'

'All right.'

Fran moved away from the desk while he made the call. She went to the window and stared across the car park while she tried to deal with what had happened. Maybe she hadn't planned on staying in the village but so long as she had somewhere to sleep, she'd be fine. She glanced round when she heard Alex replace the receiver and felt her stomach knot with nerves all over again when she saw how grim he looked.

'What's wrong? Surely they can't be fully booked? You said that they always have vacancies at this time of the year.'

'Normally they do. You'd probably have had your pick

of rooms, in fact, but it turns out that the place is closed.'
He grimaced. 'Apparently, they're having a new heating
system installed and the whole place is in a mess. Mrs
Baxter was most apologetic but she said there was no way
that she could take in any guests at the moment.'

'But I don't mind how messy it is!' Fran protested. 'I just
need a room for the weekend.'

'I understand that but Mrs Baxter was adamant. There are
floorboards up all over the place and I think she's worried
about losing her licence if she takes you in while the place
is in such a dangerous state. There's no way that she'll risk
that happening so it looks as though we're back to square
one.'

'What about the cottage?' Fran suggested desperately.
'It's going to be my home eventually so surely there's no
problem about me using the place a little earlier than
planned.'

'You can't possibly stay in the cottage! You saw the state
the place was in and there's no way that I'm allowing you
to sleep there.' He shook his head when she opened her
mouth to protest that she didn't mind the conditions, although the thought of those spiders wasn't very appealing.
'No, Francesca, it's out of the question. You'll have to stay
with me. It's the only sensible solution.'

'Oh, no, really, I couldn't,' she began, appalled by the
thought of spending the weekend under his roof when she'd
planned on keeping well away from him.

'Don't be silly. Of course you can.' He smiled at her.
'Although I can't promise you five-star luxury, at least
you'll be comfortable, plus it will give you time to look
around the village. Now that you've decided to move here
to live, it will be a good opportunity to get some idea of
what the place is really like.'

He seemed to take her agreement for granted as he dug
in his pocket and held up a bunch of keys. 'Why don't you

go and let yourself in while I finish off here? The large key opens the front door although we normally use the back door because it's easier. That's this little key with the loop on the top.'

'But I don't know where you live,' she protested as he pressed the keys into her hand. Everything seemed to be moving so fast that she felt as though she was floundering as she was carried along by the flow.

'Sorry. Stupid of me to forget the most important bit, isn't it?'

He grinned at her and Fran felt a little knot of heat form in the pit of her stomach when she saw the warmth in his eyes. She looked away but there was no point pretending that she didn't know what it meant. Alex had smiled at her like a man smiled at a woman whom he found very attractive and although part of her longed to respond, the more cautious side knew it would be a mistake. It made it very hard to stand there while he gave her directions when she was in such turmoil.

'You're quite sure that you know where you're going now?'

'I think so.' Fran took a quick breath when he came to the end of his instructions. 'Turn left after I leave the surgery then first right and your house is at the end of the lane.'

'That's right. The hall lamp is on a timer so the house won't be in total darkness when you get there. There's nothing worse than trying to find your way around a strange place in the dark, is there?'

He didn't wait for her to answer as he carried on. 'There's plenty of food in the fridge so make yourself something to eat if you're hungry. We'll sort out what else you'll need when I get home.'

'What else I'll need?'

'Toothbrush, toiletries, a change of clothes—that sort of thing.' He regarded her thoughtfully. 'Good job you're quite tall because at least my jeans won't bury you. I'll hunt you out a pair when I get back, plus a sweater and something to sleep in. The only problem then will be undies but you might be able to find something to fit you in the post office. They sell all sorts of things besides stamps,' he added with a chuckle.

'Oh, I see. Right.'

Suddenly Fran couldn't wait to leave if only to escape from the decidedly uncomfortable topic of her underwear. Heat swept up her face as she hurried to the door.

'You can leave the back door on the latch,' Alex called after her and she nodded to show that she'd heard him although she didn't look round.

She left the consulting room and made her way along the corridor. Thankfully, Mary was on the phone so Fran just waved to her before she left. She couldn't have faced telling the receptionist that she was spending the night with Alex. It was bad enough not having a choice in the matter but it would be infinitely worse if everyone in the village found out and started gossiping. She'd come to Teedale to get away from that kind of attention and the last thing she wanted was to find herself the cynosure of all eyes again.

She sighed as she left the surgery and headed along the road because moving to the country was turning out to be rather more eventful than she'd hoped it would be.

Almost an hour passed before Alex was finally able to shut up shop for the night. Although there were only two patients waiting to be seen they were both eager to hear about the new doctor who had joined the practice. He tried to keep it brief by explaining that Dr Goodwin was moving from a practice in London, but that seemed to arouse even more interest.

As he fielded questions about why Francesca had decided to leave the city, he realised that she'd never actually given him a reason apart from the fact that she wanted somewhere quiet to live. He couldn't help thinking that it was rather odd that such a young and beautiful woman had chosen to bury herself in the country and made up his mind to find out more about her reasons for doing so as soon as he had the chance.

He sent Mary home and locked up, making sure the alarm was set before he left. Although Teedale was normally a peaceful little village, there'd been a spate of burglaries recently. He made a mental note to warn Francesca to be careful about locking up then wondered if it would be a mistake to overstate the need for caution. The last thing he wanted was to scare her off—for a number of reasons.

He sighed as he drew up in front of his house because once again his mind was racing ahead of itself. He should just be grateful that he'd found someone to work in the practice instead of letting any other issues surface. So maybe Francesca was beautiful and talented but he'd been on the receiving end of all those chilly looks and not even the world's biggest optimist could imagine they'd been intended as a come-on!

Alex was still chuckling when he let himself into the kitchen only to come to a sudden halt at the sight that greeted him. Francesca was standing by the stove and he couldn't stop his mind swooping back to the days when he'd come home and found Trish standing in the very same spot. The memory was so vivid that a wave of longing swept through him for what he'd lost. It took a tremendous amount of effort to pretend everything was fine when Francesca glanced round.

'I see you found the place all right,' he said rather thickly, tossing his coat over a chair.

'Yes.' She treated him to one of trade-mark chilly looks. 'I also took advantage of your offer to make myself something to eat. I hope that was all right?'

'Of course it was. I wouldn't have suggested it if I hadn't meant it,' he said briskly, going over to the kettle. 'Fancy a cup of coffee?'

'I'd prefer tea if you have it.' She put down the spoon she'd been using and he was surprised to see a trace of nervousness on her face. 'Are you sure you don't mind me staying here? I really don't want to impose so if it's a problem then I'll find somewhere else. Maybe there's a hotel in Beesley…'

She tailed off and Alex felt his heart fill with tenderness when he saw her bite her lip. It was so unlike her to betray any sign of nervousness that he forgot about his own feelings in the need to reassure her.

'It isn't a problem. *Really.* It's my fault that you ended up stuck here so if anyone should be apologising, it should be me.'

He smiled at her, feeling his spirits lift when she gave him a tentative smile in return. Flushed with success, he hurried on. 'In fact, I can feel a good old-fashioned grovel coming on right this very minute if you'd like to hear it?'

She burst out laughing, a richly sensuous sound that made the tiny hairs all over his body spring to attention. 'No, it's OK. I shall take it as read.' She turned back to the stove and gave the contents of the saucepan another brisk stir. 'This is almost ready now so would you like some? There's enough for two.'

'What is it?' Alex asked, moving over to the stove because it seemed safer to concentrate on his stomach than the rest of his body.

'Just a can of soup with some bits and bobs added to it.' She glanced up and his breath caught when her eyes tangled with his and he saw the warmth they held. 'It's my version of stew—maximum flavour for minimum effort.'

'Sounds good to me,' he murmured because it shocked him that he could respond like this. Since Trish had died, he'd put his emotions on ice. It hadn't been difficult because he'd been far too busy looking after Daniel to think about his own needs, yet the minute he'd looked into Francesca's eyes, he'd felt his body stir to life. He hurried on, desperate to get a grip on himself before she realised something was wrong.

'You'll have to give me the recipe. My cooking tends to be a bit limited, I'm afraid. Fish fingers and chips, sausages and beans...that sort of thing.'

'I'm certainly no whiz in the kitchen,' she denied, opening cupboards to find the soup bowls. 'My cooking tends to be dictated by speed most of the time. The faster I can have something ready to eat, the more I enjoy it. Paul's always been a much better cook than me.'

'Paul?' Alex queried, wishing he'd had time to prepare himself before she'd slid the name into the conversation. He took the bowls from her, hoping she couldn't tell how deflated he felt although he really shouldn't be surprised that there was a man in her life. A woman as beautiful and as desirable as Francesca was bound to have admirers.

'Just someone I used to know,' she explained in a tone that positively crackled with ice.

Alex knew it was meant to deter him and that in other circumstances it would have worked, too, but for some reason he seemed immune at that moment. So maybe his inner voice was telling him to back off but he didn't *want* to heed the advice. He wanted to know who this Paul fellow was and why she had gone all frosty the moment his name had cropped up. Maybe he would regret this but...

'Know as in the biblical sense?' he asked with a directness that normally would have been alien to him.

'I really don't think it's any of—'

'My business?' He sighed. 'You're right. It isn't. In fact, a question like that definitely oversteps the accepted boundaries between employer and employee. All I can say in my

defence is that I'm not asking to be nosy but because I want
to know who this man is and why you froze up as soon as
you mentioned his name. However, it's your choice whether
or not you tell me. You certainly don't have to.'

He touched her lightly on the arm, felt her skin ripple
under his fingers as nerve endings fired out warning signals,
and moved away because he didn't want her to think that
he was trying to press her for information. He went over to
the cupboard and took out a couple of mugs. Francesca was
still standing by the stove and he grimaced as he dropped a
teabag into each mug because he'd overstepped the mark
by miles and not just inches. She would probably leave once
the weekend was over and it would be his own fault, too,
because he'd had no right to start probing into her affairs...

'Have you any bread to go with this?'

Her voice was still distinctly chilly but Alex let out a
whooshing sigh of relief. 'At least you're still talking to me,'
he said with a wry little grimace as he went to the bread
bin and took out the loaf that he'd bought that lunchtime.

'Just.' She shot him a vinegary look as she began spooning soup into the bowls.

'Better than nothing,' he observed lightly, plonking the
loaf onto the bread board.

He collected the butter from the fridge and took everything into the dining room then went back to fetch the china
and cutlery. It had been a long time since he'd laid the
dining-room table because Daniel had his tea at the child-
minder's house after school while he had his supper off a
tray in front of the television. It was only at weekends that
he cooked for them and then they ate in the kitchen.

Now the familiarity of setting the table for a grown-up
meal made his heart ache just a little because it reminded
him of suppertimes with Trish. And yet, oddly, he no longer
felt that overpowering sense of loss he'd experienced before.
His mind had dealt with the memory now and had stored it

away with the rest of the mementoes of his life with Trish. It made him feel a bit odd to know that the last few ties had been severed so he was glad when Francesca appeared with the food.

'That smells good,' he said, sniffing appreciatively. 'What's in it exactly?'

'A can of mushroom soup, some left-over chicken out of the fridge, plus some herbs that I found by the back door.'

She sat down and dipped her spoon into the bowl, her lips puckering enticingly as she blew on the steaming liquid to cool it.

'I didn't know we had any herbs,' Alex muttered because he had to say something otherwise he'd just sit there and stare. Francesca would think he was some kind of pervert if he sat there staring at her. She'd probably report him to the GMC and he couldn't have blamed her if she had because the thoughts he was currently entertaining weren't the sort one should harbour about a brand-new colleague!

He hurriedly dunked his spoon into the bowl and gulped down a mouthful of the soup with scant regard for its temperature so that his eyes watered when the hot liquid seared the back of his throat. He spluttered in pain and Francesca leapt to her feet.

'What have you done?' She didn't bother waiting for him to answer as she ran to the kitchen and came back with a glass of water. 'Quick, drink this before your throat blisters.'

Alex drank, feeling like a complete and total idiot. 'What a stupid thing to do,' he murmured, dredging up a smile. 'It smells so delicious that I forgot how hot it was.'

'You'd better let it cool down before you eat any more,' she warned him, reaching for the bread. She buttered a slice, delicately licking a smear of butter off her finger and almost causing him to commit the exact same act of folly all over again.

Alex breathed deeply, determined to subdue his rioting

libido. The delights of lips being puckered and fingers being licked hadn't featured in his thoughts for years. If anyone had asked, he would have said that he was past the stage of fantasising about a woman like that, but obviously not. His imagination was having a field day, dreaming up a whole raft of situations in which Francesca's lips and tongue could be put to full use, and it was both scary and exciting to realise that he could still function on this level. He realised that he needed a distraction and briskly changed the subject to something more mundane.

'How's the bread? I bought it at the local bakery. I always think their bread tastes miles better than the stuff they sell in the supermarket,' he explained brightly, inwardly groaning because he sounded like some half-witted advertising executive.

'It's delicious,' she replied, popping another piece into her mouth. 'You're lucky to have such a good baker in a small village like this.'

'We are.' Alex averted his eyes as she daintily chewed the morsel of bread because there was only so much temptation a man could stand. 'Most of the villages around here have lost all their shops but we still have the baker's and the post office. There's also a mobile butcher's van which visits twice a week and one of the local farmers sells home-grown produce so you definitely won't starve. The only problem you'll have is buying clothes—you'll have to go to Derby or Sheffield for those.'

'I doubt I'll be buying any new clothes in the forseeable future. I have other priorities at the moment.'

Alex frowned because there'd been a definite *something* in her voice when she'd said that. 'Dare I ask what sort of priorities or have I pushed my luck enough for one evening?'

She shrugged. 'It's not a secret. I want to save as much

money as I can towards the deposit on a house. I hate having to rent property and I'd like to buy something in the village.'

'So you can't see yourself going back to London at some point?' he asked, his curiosity piqued because it sounded as though she was severing all ties with her former life.

'No. I've had enough of London. I want to put down some roots and make a fresh start.'

'And you think you've found the right place to do it here in Teedale?' he asked, his spirits soaring because she obviously saw herself living in the village for some time to come.

'It's as good as anywhere else.'

'As good as anywhere else?' he repeated in astonishment. 'You're not exactly bubbling over with enthusiasm, are you?'

'No.' A wash of colour touched her cheeks but she met his eyes without flinching. 'It makes very little difference to me where I live. I just want to do my job and get on with my life.'

'Then all I can say, Francesca, is that I feel really sorry for you. Everyone deserves to have choices even if those choices don't amount to much more than where you want to live.'

He reached across the table and squeezed her hand. Maybe his only concern should have been the difference it was going to make to his life, having her working in the practice, but he couldn't help feeling upset about what she'd said.

'You deserve that choice as well, Francesca, and I don't think you should settle for living here if it isn't what you really want to do. If you ever change your mind about this job, I promise that I won't try to stop you leaving. Don't think that you have to stay just because you've signed a contract.'

'Thank you.'

She withdrew her hand and stood up but he didn't try to stop her. He'd heard the catch in her voice and knew how much she would hate him to see that she was upset. He made himself stay where he was as she gathered up her dishes although what he really wanted to do was to take her in his arms and kiss her better.

It was sheer torture to have to pretend to eat while she carried her dishes to the kitchen but this time *he* was the one who didn't have a choice. A couple more spoonfuls of soup had slithered down his throat before she returned and he was both relieved and resigned when he saw that the chill was back in her eyes. The beautiful Dr Goodwin had herself firmly under control once more.

'I think I'll have an early night,' she announced.

'Of course. You must be tired after the busy day you've had,' Alex replied evenly, standing up. 'The guest room is at the top of the stairs on the right. There's an *en suite* bathroom so you won't need to trek through the house in the middle of the night. All you need now is something to wear to sleep in. How about if I hunt out a clean T-shirt for you. Would that do?'

'Please, don't bother. I'll be perfectly fine the way I am.'

'Are you sure?'

He couldn't help himself as his eyes skimmed over her elegant black suit. What she had on didn't look like the kind of thing one could wear to bed so he could only assume that she didn't intend to wear anything at all. The thought of her lying naked between his serviceable poly-cotton sheets sent a rush of blood to his head and he bit back a groan. He really had to put the brakes on his imagination before it got him into trouble!

'Quite sure.' Twin spots of colour blazed in her cheeks as she turned and headed for the door. 'Goodnight.'

'Goodnight,' he repeated dutifully, deeming it safer to stick to basics.

He sat down after she'd left the room although there was no way he could eat another morsel of food. Pushing away the bowl, he listened while she click-clacked her way along the parquet flooring in the hall. The house was over two hundred years old and the creaking of the old timbers was something he'd long ago learned to ignore, yet his heartbeat quickened when he heard the bottom stair creak, speeded up even more when he heard a second and a third creak in rapid succession. By the time she reached the landing, he was feeling positively dizzy and it didn't end there. The guest-room door had always been stiff; now the grating of wood rubbing against wood wrung a moan from his lips…

Alex shot to his feet and hurried into the kitchen, turning on the taps so the noise of the water would mask any other sounds coming from upstairs. He would drive himself mad if he sat there imagining what was happening in the room above. Picturing Francesca getting ready for bed wasn't going to be the trailer before the main feature because there *wasn't* a main feature. She was his guest, not a prospective lover—his guest and his new colleague. Either or both of those ruled out the other!

CHAPTER FOUR

FRAN was woken by the sound of the telephone ringing. Reaching over to the bedside table, she picked up her watch and peered at the dial. Five o'clock, which probably meant it wasn't a social call.

She sighed as she climbed out of bed and pulled on the robe she'd found hanging behind the bathroom door because she would have to get used to being woken at all hours of the night from now on. Alex had told her that he didn't use an on-call service so they would probably share any out-of-hours calls between them. It was going to be hard to drag herself out of bed in the middle of the night but she'd done it during her GP rotation and she could do it again. It was just something else she would have to adjust to when she moved to the village.

The hall light was on when she arrived downstairs. She could hear noises coming from the study so she headed in that direction, feeling her heart kick in an extra beat when she spotted Alex crouched down beside the desk. She'd never taken much notice of how he'd looked the day before because she'd been too stressed about the interview and it came as a shock to suddenly realise how handsome he was. With that thick, dark hair cut close to his well-shaped head and those strongly defined features, Alex Shepherd possessed the kind of rugged good looks that could turn any woman's head and it worried her to discover that she wasn't immune to his appeal.

'Anything I can do to help?' she asked more sharply than she'd intended because letting herself get carried away by

43

her new boss's looks certainly wasn't the right way to set about rebuilding her life.

He shot to his feet, yelping in pain when he banged his head on the edge of the desk. 'You scared the living daylights out of me!' he exclaimed, rubbing his head. 'I didn't hear you coming downstairs.'

'Sorry,' Fran apologised coolly although it was hard to stop herself rushing over to check that he wasn't badly hurt. 'Next time I'll cough when I get to the bottom of the stairs.'

'Oh, I wouldn't worry about it, if I were you. I'll probably still end up braining myself.' He smiled ruefully. 'Clumsy is my middle name.'

Fran frowned because the contrast between Alex's reaction and what Paul would have done in similar circumstances was so marked that it felt as though a light had been switched on. Paul would have made a real song and dance about it, she realised. He would have gone on and on until she'd managed to apologise enough to appease him. She couldn't believe that she'd put up with such childish behaviour and it just seemed to prove once again how stupid she'd been. It was hard to hide her dismay and Alex must have noticed something was wrong.

'Hey, it really doesn't matter.' He smiled at her but she could see the concern in his eyes. 'I survived far worse than this when I was playing rugby at uni. You try having an eighteen-stone rugby player dancing on your head and then you'll *really* know what pain is!'

Despite herself, Fran chuckled. 'Doesn't sound like a whole lot of fun to me.'

'Trust me, it isn't.'

He gave her another quick smile then stooped down again. It was obvious that he was giving her a moment to collect herself and she was grateful to him for that. She hated losing control and it was even worse when she was with Alex because he had a way of making her want to tell him things. Her lips snapped together because there was no way that she was going to forget her rule about keeping her distance from him.

'I'm sure it's in here somewhere.' Alex's voice was muffled as he delved into the bottom drawer and Fran frowned.

'What exactly are you looking for?'

'A spare birthing kit.'

He glanced round and she felt a frisson run through her when their eyes met and she saw the awareness in his. Even though he was busily engaged in his search, he was still aware of her, and it was both scary and exciting to realise it.

'I know there's one in the surgery but I thought I'd save myself a journey. By the time I drive over there and go through all the rigmarole of turning off the alarms, I could be on my way to the call.'

'So it's a baby on its way, is it?' she asked, determined to stay focused.

'Yes. Marie Fisher at Boundary Farm. Her husband just phoned to say that she's having contractions. It's her third child and she was booked for a home delivery but, as luck would have it, the community midwife has been called out to another patient so Jim phoned me... Aha. Eureka!'

He stood up, grinning broadly as he deposited the kit on the desk. 'Brilliant! Now all I need is my coat and car keys then I can be on my way. From what Jim was saying, everything seems to be moving pretty fast so I'd hate the baby to get there before I do.'

'Shall I come with you?' Fran offered, rather surprised by the sudden excitement she felt. Of course it was the prospect of helping to deliver a new baby, she assured herself, and had nothing to do with her wanting to be with Alex.

'There's no need...' he began then stopped. 'Actually, it would be great to have you along. Although I'm not anticipating any problems, you just never know, do you? Another pair of hands could be very useful.'

'I'll get dressed, then,' she told him, swinging round. She hurried along the hall then paused when he called to her.

'It's pouring down outside so you'll need something a bit more substantial to wear than that suit. I'll see what I can find to fit you.' He followed her along the hall. 'And you'll need a pair of wellies, too. They're the one fashion accessory no self-respecting GP can do without in this part of the world.'

'Fine. Whatever,' Fran agreed, leading the way upstairs because there wasn't time to debate the issue.

Alex went straight to his bedroom and began hauling open drawers. 'This should do and this… Oh, and you'd better have these as well. The jeans will probably be too long on you but you can roll up the hems.'

Fran gulped as he piled an assortment of his clothing onto the bed. She would have dearly loved to refuse to wear it only she couldn't afford to make an issue of it in case he started wondering why. How could she explain that the thought of wearing his clothes next to her skin was making her break out in goose-bumps?

'Thanks.'

She bundled everything together and hurried back to her room, refusing to think about why she'd reacted so strongly to the idea. Fortunately, she'd rinsed out her underwear before she'd gone to bed and hung it on the radiator to dry so at least that was clean. She slipped on the familiar silk panties and bra then steeled herself as she pulled a clean white T-shirt over her head. The fabric smelled faintly of detergent but that was all and she breathed a sigh of relief because there was no trace of Alex on the fabric. Five minutes later she arrived back downstairs to find him waiting for her by the front door with a waxed jacket and a pair of Wellington boots.

'My sister left these here for when she next comes to stay,' he explained, handing her the jacket. 'She's about your size so they should fit.'

'Thanks.' Fran slid her arms into the jacket and zipped up the front then pushed her feet into the rubber boots. 'They're fine. A perfect fit, in fact.'

'Excellent!' Alex laughed as he opened the door and swept her a bow. 'Come along then, Cinderella, it's time to go to the ball!'

Fran didn't say anything as she got into the car although Alex had got the fairy story the wrong way round. Checking if the shoe had fitted had come *after* Cinderella had been to the ball—when the prince had come to carry her back to his castle. The story always ended there so there was no proof that the couple had lived happily ever after. Maybe they, too, had discovered that love didn't last.

A feeling of sadness suddenly enveloped her because if she could no longer believe in love, what could she believe in?

'It wasn't like this with the other two. She popped out our Harry and our Emily as though it were no harder than shelling peas! I tell you, Dr Shepherd, something's gone wrong this time.'

'I'm sure everything will be fine, Jim.' Alex patted Jim Fisher on the shoulder, hoping the man's fears would prove groundless because he could do without a medical emergency on his hands. He glanced round when Francesca came to join them, summoning a smile as he introduced her to the farmer.

The drive to Boundary Farm had been completed in a silence that had positively reeked of tension. In other circumstances, he would have stopped the car and demanded to know what was wrong, but he knew that Francesca would have rebuffed his attempts to find out what was worrying her. He sighed because it hurt to know that she was determined to keep him at arm's length.

'Right, let's get inside and see how Marie's doing.' He swiftly returned his thoughts to the reason why they were there as he ushered Francesca ahead of him into the farmhouse. There was a fire burning in the kitchen grate and he sighed appreciatively as he hung his coat behind the door. 'At least it's nice and warm in here. It's really rough outside tonight.'

'They've forecast snow,' Jim told him glumly. 'That's all we need, isn't it? It'll be a nightmare if we have to get Marie to hospital in the middle of a snowstorm.'

'Let's not get ahead of ourselves,' Alex said firmly. 'We don't know if there's a problem yet so let's wait until I've examined Marie before we start with the worst-case scenarios. Is she upstairs?'

'Aye, and you're right too, Dr Shepherd. There's no point borrowing trouble, is there?' Jim took Francesca's coat and hung it on a peg then led them along the hall. 'Marie's in the front bedroom so go on up. I just want to check how the little ones are doing. I brought them downstairs in case they got upset, not that they seem the least bit bothered, mind. They think it's great fun being woken up to watch a video!'

'I bet they do,' Alex agreed, smiling as he turned to Francesca. 'Shall we go on up and take a look, then?'

'Of course,' she replied coolly, leading the way up the stairs.

He sighed as he followed her because if he'd hoped her attitude might have softened after a night spent under his roof, he'd been sadly mistaken. It made him wonder what it would take to break through the barrier she'd erected around herself and if he would ever manage to do it. Was it just him she was so wary of, or men in general?

It was a disquieting thought and he tried to put it out of

his mind as they went into the bedroom. Marie was lying on the bed and it was obvious that she was in a great deal of pain.

'You look worn out, Marie,' he said, going straight over to the bed. 'Is the pain really bad?'

'Awful. It's much worse than when I had Harry or Emily,' she replied, then stopped as another contraction began.

Alex waited until the contraction had finished before he examined her, his spirits plummeting at what he found. Although Marie was fully dilated there was no sign of the head crowning and he doubted if there would be either. Taking the special fetal stethoscope out of the birthing kit, he listened to the baby's heartbeat, wishing that he had an electronic fetal monitor at hand, not to mention all the other equipment available in a modern maternity unit. Francesca was watching him and he nodded to her after he finished his examination by checking Marie's blood pressure.

'See what you think.'

She moved to the bed and introduced herself. 'I'm Francesca Goodwin, Dr Shepherd's new partner. I apologise for the way I'm dressed but, to cut a long story short, I hadn't planned on spending the weekend in Teedale so I had to borrow some of Alex's clothes.' She lowered her voice. 'Suffice to say that he chose them for me.'

Despite her discomfort, Marie chuckled. 'Enough said, Dr Goodwin. Men haven't a clue when it comes to clothes, have they?'

'They certainly haven't. And make that Francesca.'

One last smile before she began her examination but it was more than enough to make Alex's head spin. The fact that Francesca behaved so *warmly* towards a patient just seemed to highlight how coldly she behaved towards him. Did she perceive him as a threat, perhaps?

'I see what you mean.'

Her tone was bland enough but he was too attuned to its nuances to miss the underlying anxiety it held. He nodded towards the door, needing to speak to her out of Marie's hearing while they ran through their options. She excused herself, her grey eyes betraying her concern as she joined him.

'The baby's lying horizontally. No wonder Marie's having such a struggle to deliver it. It's arm and shoulder must be jammed in her pelvis.'

'There's no way it can be born from that position.'

'So what are our options?'

'Extremely limited, I'm afraid.' He grimaced. 'It will take an hour for an ambulance to get here and that's without allowing for the current weather conditions.'

'And another hour to get Marie to hospital.' She shook her head. 'That's far too long to wait. The baby's already getting distressed and I'm not happy with Marie's blood pressure either. It's higher than it should be.'

'Which means we'll have to deliver the baby ourselves. When did you last perform a Caesarean section, Doctor?'

'During my training. One of my rotations was in the maternity unit at Dalverston General Hospital. I helped deliver a child by Caesarean section then.'

Alex whistled. 'At least you chose the right place to gain your experience. Dalverston's maternity unit is one of the best in the country.'

'It is but it's going to be vastly different delivering a baby here.'

'It will but we'll manage,' he said firmly.

'Are you sure? Surely there's a risk of infection setting in if we operate under non-sterile conditions.'

'There is but we'll do everything we can to safeguard against it happening. We really don't have a choice, Francesca. Both the baby and Marie could die if we wait any longer. If it's any consolation, I've done a couple of sections over the years and they've been fine so there's no reason why this one shouldn't be, too.'

It wasn't a lie; however, the first had been performed under supervision during his training and on the second occasion he'd had Trish to assist him. They'd worked together to deliver that baby and he could still remember the rush of emotion they'd experienced afterwards and how it had crystallised the tentative plans they'd made to start their own family. Daniel had been born almost nine months to the day after that delivery and it was a poignant reminder of his past life—which he couldn't afford to dwell on when Marie was in desperate need of his help. Galvanised by the thought, he started rattling out instructions.

'Can you ask Jim to phone for an ambulance? Even though it won't get here before we deliver the baby, we need to know that it's on its way. Then can you find some place to perform the operation? It's far too dark in here. We need to be able to see what we're doing so can you find somewhere where there's enough decent lighting?'

'How about the kitchen? It was very bright in there and warm, too. I also noticed there was a big old farmhouse table which would be ideal for our purposes.'

'Good idea!' he exclaimed, relieved that she seemed to have conquered her misgivings and was as determined as he was to give it their best shot. 'Can you sort everything out while I explain what's happened to Marie? It's bound to be a shock for her.'

'Leave it to me,' Francesca said, hurrying to the door.

Alex's mouth tilted as he heard her running down the stairs because he didn't doubt that she'd soon have everything organised. They were on the same wavelength when it came to work, both of them able to cut through the nonessentials and home in on the crux of a problem. She'd been exactly the same yesterday when he'd dumped that surgery on her. She'd coped and she'd coped well, too, not just scraped by as so many would have done. When it came to her work it was maximum effort for maximum results— unlike her cooking!

He chuckled because it felt remarkably good to have a little inside knowledge about what made her tick.

'There's no need to worry, Marie. The anaesthetic will block any really bad pain.'

Fran squeezed the woman's hand, knowing how scary this must be for her. She looked up as Alex turned off the taps after scrubbing his hands, wondering slightly hysterically how she'd found herself in this situation. Delivering babies on kitchen tables was way beyond her experience and she couldn't help thinking they were mad to attempt it.

'I'll need you to monitor Marie once I've administered the anaesthetic.'

Alex snapped on a pair of gloves as he came over to the table and she took a steadying breath because she didn't want him to think that she couldn't cope.

'What are you going to use as an anaesthetic agent?' she asked as calmly as she could.

'This.' He showed her the drug. 'It's a highly effective analgesic, plus there isn't the problem of maintaining an airway, which makes it ideal in this instance. Marie will be unconscious but she'll be able to breathe on her own.'

'Have you used it before?' Fran asked curiously because he seemed very confident.

'Several times. The area around Teedale is very popular with cavers and it's amazing how often they find themselves in trouble. I'm part of the cave rescue team and we often get called out to people who've injured themselves. Last summer, for instance, we had to rescue a young man who'd broken both his legs. He was in tremendous pain but we were able to get him out after I'd made him comfortable with a shot of this. The analgesic effect of the drug is double that of morphine.'

'Caving?' She shuddered. 'I can't understand why anyone would want to take it up as a hobby.'

'It's not my idea of a fun pastime either, but a lot of people enjoy it.'

'So you're only involved because of your position as GP in this district?' she asked, her heart sinking at the thought that she might have to assist if there was an incident requiring medical intervention.

'That's right. There were a couple of really bad accidents not long after I moved here and I got roped in to help. I ended up doing the training because it made sense to have an idea of what I was doing. However, I certainly don't expect you to get involved. It definitely isn't part of your job description if that's what you're worried about.'

'Thank heavens for that!' she exclaimed, and he laughed.

'Sorry, I didn't mean to scare you. So now that we've cleared that up, shall we get this show on the road?'

'Oh, yes, definitely. The sooner the better, in fact.' She looked at Marie and smiled. 'Mind you, I'm not the one getting a needle stuck into me, am I?'

'Chicken feed compared to everything else that's happening,' Marie panted, riding out another contraction.

Fran squeezed her hand. 'You're a real star. I bet you never imagined your baby would be delivered on the kitchen table, did you?'

'I certainly didn't. Still, it's as good a place as any, isn't it, Jim?'

She reached for her husband's hand and Fran turned away because she found it unbearably moving to see the loving look the couple exchanged. She quickly swabbed Marie's arm in readiness for the anaesthetic then looked up when Alex said softly, 'Everything OK?'

Heat swept up her face because she knew that he wasn't

referring to their patient. He'd noticed how moved she'd been and it worried her to know how transparent she was when she wanted to hide her feelings.

'Fine. Why shouldn't it be?'

'No reason at all.'

He gave her a quick smile but she saw the disappointment in his eyes and knew that he'd been hurt by her deliberate rebuff. Maybe she didn't want to get involved with him but was that a good enough reason to be so prickly when he was trying to be kind?

'Sorry.' She gave a little shrug when he glanced at her. 'Just nerves, I expect.'

'Everything will be fine, Francesca. You'll see.'

He didn't say anything else as he administered the injection and Fran was glad to let the subject drop. The drug soon took effect and once Marie was unconscious, Alex made an incision in her abdomen just above her pubic bone then carefully cut through the lower part of her uterus. It took just a few minutes to deliver the baby after that and Fran wrapped the infant in a towel while Alex removed the afterbirth. It was a little boy and perfectly healthy, too, if his strident cries were anything to go by.

'You've got a beautiful little boy,' she told Jim. 'Just let me clean him up a bit then you can hold him.'

'A boy?' Jim repeated. 'But we thought it was going to be another girl!'

Fran laughed as she started drying the baby with a towel. 'We can always put him back if you don't want him.'

'No way!' Jim laughed. 'Not after what we've just been through to get him.'

'So long as you're happy,' she teased. She wrapped the baby in a blanket that had been warming in front of the fire then placed him in his father's arms. 'Here he is. The latest addition to the Fisher family.'

'He's beautiful.' Jim kissed the top of his new son's head

and his eyes were brimming with tears of happiness. 'Really beautiful. Just like his mum.'

Fran felt a lump come to her throat and turned away before she made a fool of herself. Alex was starting to sew up so she helped him then dressed the incision. Marie soon came round from the anaesthetic so Fran tidied her up then went to fetch the children so they could meet their new brother. They'd decided not to move Marie until the ambulance arrived so she and Alex went into the hall to give the family some time together.

'Am I glad that's over.' He huffed out a sigh as he sank down onto the stairs.

'Me, too.' Fran sat down beside him. 'You did a brilliant job just now, Alex.'

'Thank you, but I couldn't have managed it without your help.' He smiled at her, his eyes full of something that made her heart suddenly race. 'We work very well together, don't we?'

'So it appears,' she agreed as calmly as she could.

'Oh, Fran, what *am* I going to do with you?' He shook his head in despair. 'You always have to qualify every statement, don't you? It *appears* we work well together, meaning there's an element of doubt. I wonder what it would take to stop you holding back all the time.'

'I don't know what you mean,' she denied, scrambling to her feet. 'I'd better go and check on Marie…'

'Marie is fine, as you very well know. You're just using her as an excuse to avoid answering the question.'

He leant back on his elbows and regarded her thoughtfully, as though he was trying to work out the answer to a very complicated puzzle. 'I find it really hard to understand you, Fran. I watched you with Marie before and you were wonderful with her—warm, caring, really sympathetic—yet you seem to put up a barrier whenever we talk and deliberately freeze me out. It makes me wonder if you have a problem with men in general or if it's just me who has this effect on you. To be honest, I think it's going to be very difficult for us to work together if it's the latter so maybe we need to sort this out right now.'

CHAPTER FIVE

FRAN really, really didn't want to answer that question but she could tell from Alex's expression that she didn't have a choice.

'I don't have a problem with you, Alex. I've made a lot of changes to my life recently and I just need some time to myself to sort everything out.' She shrugged, hoping to play down the situation. 'It's easier with the patients because there's already a certain…*distance* between us.'

'I see. And is there anything I can do to help?'

'Not really…apart from being patient with me.'

She bit her lip because she hadn't intended to add that rider and could only hope he wouldn't read too much into it. She made her way back to the kitchen and checked Marie's blood pressure, took another look at the baby then tidied away the equipment they'd used. She knew that she was keeping busy because she didn't want to think about the possibility of forming another relationship with a man. It simply wasn't going to happen although she didn't want to have to explain that to Alex. It was a relief when the wail of a siren announced that the ambulance had arrived because it provided a welcome distraction.

Alex came into the kitchen and shrugged on his coat, his expression betraying very little when he turned to her. 'I'll go and meet the ambulance while you finish off in here. The consultant at the hospital would probably appreciate a few notes if you could sort something out.'

'Of course.'

Fran treated him to a smile, feeling easier now they were back on safe ground. She quickly wrote up her report, noting down the drugs they'd used, the length of time that Marie had been anaesthetised and the condition of the baby on delivery. She did another quick BP check then added that to the report and signed it, by which time the paramedics were there. They transferred Marie to a stretcher and tucked the baby in beside her before wheeling her out to the ambulance.

Fran went with them, bending to kiss Marie's cheek before she was loaded on board. 'I'm glad everything worked out so well for you.'

'So am I. Thank you so much, Francesca,' Marie said sincerely, her eyes swimming with tears. 'I don't know what would have happened if you and Alex hadn't got here in time.'

'You just take care of yourself and that gorgeous little boy,' Fran told her mistily because it was an emotional moment for all of them.

'I shall.'

Marie hugged the baby to her as the paramedics loaded her on board. Once that was done, Fran handed over her report and a few minutes later the ambulance set off. There was a collective sigh as they watched it drive away.

'That's that, then,' Alex said briskly, leading the way back to the house.

'Aye. I've just got to take this pair to my mother's then I'll follow on to the hospital,' Jim told them. 'I know Marie has thanked you but I just want to add my thanks as well. I'm truly grateful for what you both did. You probably saved Marie's life as well as the baby's and I'll never forget that.'

'It was our pleasure,' Alex said warmly. 'Wasn't it, Fran?'

'Yes,' she murmured because she still felt a bit choked by it all.

Alex unhooked her coat from the peg and held it out for her. 'Time we were on our way, I think.'

She slid her arms into the sleeves, stiffening when she felt his hands grip her shoulders for a moment before he released her and opened the door. She followed him outside, joining in as they said their goodbyes, but that brief touch had unsettled her even more. The feel of his strong hands had sent a wave of longing through her but she couldn't afford to lean on him, professionally or personally. She had to be strong or risk suffering the consequences all over again.

Alex knew he shouldn't have done that. Francesca had made it clear that she didn't want anyone getting too close to her so why on earth had he squeezed her shoulders like that? Had he really thought she would appreciate the gesture of support?

His mouth thinned as he climbed into the car because he already knew the answer to that question. Fran got in beside him and he waited while she closed the door before starting the engine. A light peppering of snow was falling now and he flicked on the windscreen wipers before they set off.

'Will the snow stick, do you think?'

Her voice held a layer of tension beneath its apparent calm and he gritted his teeth. She'd told him how she intended to handle things and he'd had no right to breach the boundaries she'd drawn up.

'It might. Fortunately, most people who live around here are used to the vagaries of our weather and are prepared for it. It's the tourists who often find themselves in trouble.'

'You mean like that caver you mentioned before?'

'Yes, and hikers, hill walkers—basically anyone who's keen on outdoor activities,' he replied, feeling a little better because she sounded more interested now. Did her decision to change her life have anything to do with that Paul fellow?

he wondered then sighed because it really wasn't his business.

'The weather in the Peak District can change in the blink of an eye,' he continued, determined to stay focused. 'Spring is notorious for sudden snowfalls and if you don't have the right equipment with you, you can soon find yourself in serious trouble.'

'You'll have to give me a list of dos and don'ts. I'm more used to dealing with the possibility of being mugged than coping with the elements,' she explained wryly.

Alex laughed. 'A real townie, eh?'

'Most definitely. I've not been anywhere more remote than Green Park for the past few years so I'm not really up to speed when it comes to survival techniques.'

'It's mainly common sense, although I'll put together a list of things you should always carry in your car.'

'Thanks. I'd appreciate that.'

'No problem,' he said lightly. 'You'll also need to carry a far more comprehensive medical kit with you than you're used to. Because of the length of time it takes to get an ambulance out here, we cover any emergency calls in our area. What usually happens is that Ambulance Control phones the surgery as soon as they've dispatched an ambulance and we do what we can until it arrives. I don't need to tell you that speed is of the essence in an emergency.'

'The "golden hour",' she quoted. 'Get medical aid to a patient within an hour and you have a far greater chance of saving his life.'

'Exactly.' He turned onto the main road and picked up speed as they headed towards the village. 'We average a couple of emergency calls per month in the summer when there's a lot of visitors about so you'll need to be prepared to go out at the drop of a hat. I hope that won't be a problem for you?'

'I can't see why it should be. It's all part of the job, isn't it?'

'Yes, but some folk find it rather restricting to know they can be paged at any hour of the day or night. Obviously, I'm first on call and you'll be contacted only if I'm unavailable, which won't be very often, if it's any consolation.'

'I'm more than willing to do my fair share of the work, Alex. I certainly don't expect any favours.'

'I wasn't implying that you did,' he said quietly as he pulled up in front of his house.

'Oh.' She pursed her lips and he sighed wearily.

'Look, Fran, you have to stop being so...well, so *suspicious* of my motives. All I want is for us to be able to work together with the least amount of difficulty,' he explained, mentally crossing his fingers at the small white lie because there were other things he would very much like to do, number one on the list being to get to know her better. However, bearing in mind what she'd told him earlier, it seemed unlikely that was going to happen so he battened down his disappointment and carried on.

'I was just warning you what to expect. I don't want you to find that working here is such a shock to your system that you regret taking the job. It won't help either of us if that happens.'

'Of course not. And I apologise if you thought I was implying anything,' she said stiffly and with even more reserve than usual.

'Forget it.'

Alex swung himself out of the car because it was pointless trying to discuss the issue when the barriers were firmly raised. He let them into the house and groaned when he saw the clock.

'I didn't realise it was so late. I'll have to get a move on. I promised Daniel that I'd collect him before ten and he'll be wondering what's happened to me.'

'You don't hold a Saturday morning surgery, do you?'

'No. I cancelled it after Trish died because I needed to spend more time with Daniel. If there's an emergency then folk know they can phone me at home. We keep any appointments to weekdays and it seems to work pretty well.'

'That's fine. I was going to offer to cover for you if there was a surgery this morning, but obviously there's no need.'

'You can have the morning to yourself—maybe use the time to explore the village,' he suggested.

She shrugged. 'Maybe. We'll see.'

Alex didn't say anything else; he just excused himself and went to get changed because there was no point getting obsessed with the idea that she'd looked a little lost at the thought of spending the morning on her own. He would have offered to take her with him only he didn't want to overstep the demarcation line she'd drawn between professional courtesy and over-familiarity.

Thankfully, Daniel seemed little the worse for his ordeal and chatted happily on the drive back from the hospital, but for once Alex found his concentration wavering. He kept wondering what Francesca had been doing and hoping that she was all right. He sighed as he drew up in front of the house because it was stupid to worry about her like this. She was a grown woman and certainly wouldn't appreciate his concern.

Daniel leapt out of the car and raced into the house. Alex followed more slowly, his heart thumping at the thought of seeing Francesca again. He couldn't recall feeling this nervous since the first time he'd taken a girl out on a date and couldn't understand why it was happening now. Why on earth should she have this effect on him?

'Who's Francesca?' Daniel demanded as soon as he came through the kitchen door.

'The new doctor who's just joined the practice. I told you

about her yesterday,' he replied automatically, still trying to get his emotions in check.

'Oh, yes, I forgot.' Daniel thrust a piece of paper into his hand. 'It says she's gone back to London so I don't suppose I'll meet her today.'

Daniel didn't wait for him to answer as he went thundering out of the room. Alex stared blankly at the note for a moment before he made himself read it. It didn't take him very long because there were just a couple of lines informing him that she'd managed to find a taxi to take her to Derby from where she would catch a train to London, and that she would be in touch the following week to finalise the arrangements for starting work.

He turned the note over but there was nothing on the back, no good wishes and certainly no kisses. The note was as impersonal as Francesca herself had tried to be and he sighed because he didn't want impersonal, did he? He wanted more than that even though he wasn't prepared to quantify exactly what at the moment.

'I'm sorry to bother you, Fran, but Kathleen Price is on the phone. She wants to know if the results of her mammogram have come back?'

'I'm not sure, Mary. Just let me check.'

Fran wedged the phone against her ear as she brought up Kathleen's file onto the computer. It was only her second day in the job but so far she'd had remarkably few problems. Mary had been a big help, guiding her through the routine paperwork, and Alex had gone out of his way to make her feel welcome without invading her personal space in any way. He'd also arranged for the cottage to be cleaned and painted in readiness for her to move in and she was grateful to him for that. It was typically thoughtful of him.

'I've got the results here,' she said, determinedly focusing on the matter at hand because it wouldn't help to dwell on his kindness. 'Could you put Kathleen through, please? I'll have a word with her now.'

Fran quickly read through the report, smiling when she saw that the mammogram had shown no sign of malignancy. She relayed the good news to Kathleen as soon as the woman came on the line and heard Kathleen sigh with relief.

'Oh, that's a real weight off my mind, Dr Goodwin. I know they said they'd send me the results by post but I just couldn't wait any longer which is why I decided to phone the surgery. I hope you don't mind?'

'Of course not. And I'm delighted that you've got the all-clear,' Fran assured her warmly. She looked up when someone knocked on the door, feeling heat fizz along her veins when Alex appeared. He was wearing a khaki-green shirt that day and she couldn't help noticing how the colour made his eyes appear more green than hazel.

Her pulse leapt in alarm because she really shouldn't be noticing details like that. She beckoned him into the room then did her best to ignore him as he sat down beside her desk. Kathleen was still talking, bubbling over with delight at the good news, so she didn't interrupt her....

The chair creaked as Alex leant over and took the latest copy of one of the medical journals off her desk and she jumped. She glanced at him and flushed when he mouthed, 'Sorry.' She hurriedly looked away but it was difficult to concentrate when the rustle of paper was a constant reminder of his presence. When Kathleen started to wind down, Fran hurriedly stepped in. The sooner she ended the conversation, the sooner she could deal with whatever Alex wanted and send him on his way.

'If you have any concerns in the future, Kathleen, make an appointment to see me. As I've already mentioned, there are drugs I can prescribe if the problem gets too uncomfortable.'

Another round of thanks ensued before she was able to

hang up. Alex closed the magazine and looked expectantly at her.

'I take it that was Kathleen Price on the phone?'

'Yes. She wanted to know if the results of her mammogram had come back.'

'They arrived yesterday. I found them in my tray last night. They were addressed to me because the hospital doesn't have your name on record yet.' He grimaced. 'I was going to tell you they'd arrived but Kathleen beat me to it.'

'It doesn't matter,' she said quickly, not wanting him to think she was making an issue of it.

'Good.' He smiled at her. 'So how was your first night in the cottage? No little furry visitors, I hope?'

'Not that I noticed.' She summoned a smile in return, hoping he couldn't tell how on edge she felt. He was just being polite—updating her about a patient and making sure she was comfortable—so there was no need to panic.

'Great. I meant to tell you that I've arranged to have the place repainted whenever you want it done. I had no idea what colours you liked so decided it would be simpler to have everywhere painted white. One of the local men did it so you'll just need to tell him what you want and he'll do the rest.'

'Oh, that's very kind but there's no need to go to all that trouble on my account,' she said hastily because he'd done more than enough already. 'The white paint is fine.'

'It's no trouble. As I said, if I'd known your taste, I'd have had it done properly before you moved in.' He shrugged. 'Alan's a good worker and he's completely trustworthy so you don't need to worry about him being in the house when you're not there.'

'It isn't that. I just don't want you to think that you *have* to get the place redecorated for me,' she said stiffly.

'I'd have had it done no matter who moved in so if you've got it into your head that I'm doing it as a special

favour to you, forget it. We've already discussed the fact
that you don't want any special treatment so there's no need
to worry that there's any strings attached to the offer.'

'I wasn't,' she denied hastily.

'That's OK, then.' He didn't say anything else as he stood
up but she could tell that she'd upset him. She sighed because the last thing she wanted to do was to cause friction
between them.

'Anyway, I just popped in to ask you if we could get
together to work out a rota for the clinics. It shouldn't take
very long but we need to know who's doing what. Could
you spare me a few minutes after surgery this morning?'

'Of course,' she agreed, eager to smooth over any awk-
wardness. 'My last patient is booked in for ten-thirty. I've
a couple of people coming in for test results after that but
the first one isn't due until eleven-fifteen.'

'We'll try to fit it in then, barring any emergencies, of
course. Thanks.'

Fran sighed as he left the room because she hadn't handled things very well. Alex hadn't put a foot wrong and
there'd been no need for her to be so defensive. She got up,
feeling oddly ill at ease as she went to collect her patients'
notes. Dealing with Alex always unsettled her and she
wasn't sure why. Was it the fact that she found it harder
than she'd expected to maintain her distance from him?

'Oops!'

She stopped dead when a small boy came hurtling out of
the office and cannoned into her. 'Where are you off to in
such a hurry?' she asked, putting out a steadying hand.

'I was just going to find my dad.'

'Your dad?'

'Dr Shepherd. I'm Daniel,' he explained helpfully.

'Oh, I see.'

Now that it had been pointed out to her, she could see
the resemblance. With his dark hair and hazel eyes, the boy

was a miniature version of Alex. Despite her resolve not to get involved, she found herself smiling at him.

'Not the same Daniel who fell off a climbing frame and ended up in hospital?' she teased, and he chuckled.

'Yes! I was doing this really cool move, too.' He bent over to demonstrate. 'I had hold of the bar like this when Jack—he's my best friend—dared me to let go and I fell off.'

'So that's how it happened, is it?'

Alex had come along the corridor without them noticing and she jumped when she heard his voice. She glanced round and felt her pulse leap when he winked at her.

'I've not managed to get the full story out of this young man before. Obviously, you're better at getting to the truth than me.'

'He probably thought he'd get into trouble if he told you what had happened,' she said, determinedly keeping her tone light.

'Probably.' He placed his hand on his son's shoulder. 'But next time you feel like accepting a dare, think about your poor old dad, will you? I've enough grey hairs without you adding any more.'

Daniel giggled. 'It isn't my fault your hair's going grey. It's because you're so *old*, Dad!'

'Thanks very much!' Alex turned to Fran and rolled his eyes. 'See what I have to put up with?'

Fran burst out laughing, enjoying the interplay between father and son. 'I'm sure Daniel was only telling you the truth.'

'Not you as well!' He groaned. 'The two of you are ganging up on me now. It's not fair.'

'We wouldn't do that, would we, Daniel?' she denied loftily, smiling at the little boy.

'Course not!' Daniel declared, grinning.

Fran laughed. 'See. I told you so. It's just your paranoia surfacing.'

'Oh, is *that* what it is?'

He smiled at her and her pulse leapt again when she saw the warmth in his eyes. She turned away, feeling sick and shaken by her response. Maybe Alex wasn't anything like Paul but she didn't intend to get to know him well enough to find out.

'I'd better get ready before my patients arrive,' she murmured, easing around him.

'And I'd better get this young fellow off to school before he's late.'

His deep voice grated and a shiver ran through her because he'd obviously sensed that something had upset her.

'I'll see you later, Fran. Around ten-thirty in the staff-room.'

'Yes, fine,' she agreed, hurrying into the office. She collected the notes and took them back to her room. Sitting down at her desk, she checked the files against her list of appointments. She liked to be prepared and it was worth spending a few extra minutes, making sure everything was in order...

Her hands suddenly stilled because there was no point trying to pretend that work was uppermost on her mind at that moment. It was Alex who had the prime slot, Alex who made her feel so mixed up when she wanted to be in control. He had the strangest effect on her but she had to find a way to maintain the right balance when dealing with him. Polite but distant seemed to be the way to go. It shouldn't be that difficult because she was naturally reserved and had always preferred to take her time getting to know people.

That had been the mistake she'd made with Paul; she hadn't waited to get to know him but had fallen madly, passionately in love with him in the space of a few weeks.

It was little wonder their relationship had turned into such a disaster…

She blinked. Why on earth was she comparing her experiences with Paul to her dealings with Alex? The situation was completely different. Alex most definitely wasn't a potential lover!

CHAPTER SIX

ALEX was late finishing his morning list so it was almost eleven by the time he arrived at the staffroom. He opened the door and sighed when he realised that Francesca must have been delayed as well. It was always difficult to find the time to discuss practice matters during the day because they kept to a very tight schedule. He and Trish had often ended up working in the evening and he didn't want to get into that situation again although he might not have a choice.

'I'm sorry I'm late. I had to spend extra time with my last patient and that delayed me.'

He turned as Francesca came hurrying into the room, thinking how lovely she looked. She was dressed that day in a dove-grey cashmere sweater that matched her eyes and a knee-length black skirt which drew attention to her shapely legs. He allowed himself a brief moment of pleasure while he savoured her appearance before he returned his thoughts to practice matters, where they should have remained.

'Don't worry about it,' he said easily, plugging in the kettle. 'I only just got here myself. What was wrong with your patient?'

'She's very worried about her daughter.' Fran picked up a teatowel and dried a couple of mugs that had been left in the rack to drain. 'Apparently, the girl has been harming herself by cutting her arms.'

'Nasty,' he observed, taking a jar of instant coffee out of the cupboard. 'Who is it, by the way?'

'Angela Robinson. Her daughter's called Sarah.'

'I know who you mean although I haven't had any dealings with them yet. The family moved to Teedale just before Christmas so I haven't seen them since they came into the surgery to register. Did Angela come to see you specifically about her daughter or did she have a problem as well?'

'She's going through the menopause and been suffering badly from night sweats.' Fran took the jar of coffee from him and unscrewed the lid.

'So what did you prescribe?' he said huskily, trying to quell the shiver that had run through him when their hands had touched. 'HRT?'

'No. Angela has a family history of breast cancer so I decided not to prescribe it for her. Her mother and her aunt were both diagnosed with breast cancer in their early forties so I suggested a herbal supplement instead.' She looked pointedly at him and he could see the challenge in her eyes. 'I hope you're not against herbal medicine?'

'Not at all. I like to keep an open mind. Anyhow, I don't think it's possible to dismiss the value of herbal remedies when so many of the drugs we use today are derived from plants. We'd be in a sorry state if nobody had realised the value of aspirin or quinine, for instance.'

'Indeed.'

She reached for the kettle and he stifled a sigh because he knew her prickliness owed less to her concern about him having a closed mind than a desire to keep him at arm's length. Had she sensed his response just now when they'd touched? Or could it be that she'd experienced the same reaction? The idea shocked him so much that he had to struggle not to betray how startling he found it as she made the coffee then went to the fridge.

'Do you take milk?'

'Please.'

He managed to smile but his heart seemed to be playing leapfrog over his ribs. The thought that Francesca might be as aware of him as he was of her had almost blown him away. He took the cup from her and was about to gulp down a mouthful of coffee when she intervened.

'Careful! You don't want to scald yourself again, do you?'

'No.' He smiled wryly because he was normally the one urging caution. It just seemed to prove how susceptible he was to her and it was unsettling to admit it. 'Thanks for reminding me,' he said as lightly as he could.

'Don't mention it.' She carried her cup over to the table and, after a moment's hesitation, he joined her. She took a sip of her coffee then glanced at him.

'Anyway, to get back to Angela, once I'd sorted her out, she told me about her daughter. Apparently, Sarah has harmed herself before. She was bullied at her last school and that's when she started cutting herself. The family decided to move so they could make a fresh start and it was fine at first, but in the past few weeks Sarah has started doing it again.'

'Dealing with a situation like this is never easy. Most teenagers harm themselves because it gives them a sense of control over what's happening in their lives. They then become addicted to the release they get from cutting themselves and a cycle begins.' He sighed. 'Sarah could be finding it difficult to fit in at her new school and that's what has triggered it this time.'

'That's what I suggested to Angela but she was so upset that I'm not sure if she took it in. I've asked her to make an appointment for Sarah so we can have a chat but I don't know how much good it will do.'

'She really needs specialist help,' he said firmly. 'We can try to help her but she'll need constant support to get through this. Psychotherapy is often useful to get to the root of the problem.'

'Is there anyone I could refer her to around here? I know

there are a number of clinics in London specialising in this type of problem but are there any in this part of the country?'

'Oh, yes. We've made a lot of advances here in the past few years,' he replied, completely deadpan. 'For instance, we no longer rub warts with a potato and bury it at midnight because we've discovered some wonderful modern remedies instead.'

'I didn't mean that!' she exclaimed, and he laughed.

'I know. I just couldn't resist teasing you.'

'Oh, I see.' She gave him a tiny smile which suddenly grew into a much bigger one. 'You wretch! Here I was, thinking that I'd insulted you.'

'It takes a lot to insult me,' he told her, grinning. 'I'm the original Teflon man. Insults just slide off me.'

'I'll remember that,' she warned him, laughing.

There was a moment when their eyes met and his stomach muscles clenched when he felt the flow of emotion that passed between them. He sucked in his breath because it was almost too much to take in. For one glorious moment she had lowered her guard and reached out to him and it was the most wonderful feeling that he just had to say something.

'Look, Fran—' he began then stopped when the door opened and Mary appeared.

'I'm sorry to interrupt you, Alex, but Ambulance Control's just phoned. There's been an incident at the leisure centre in Beesley and they want to know if you can respond until the ambulances get there.'

'Ambulances?' he queried, immediately rising to his feet. 'It must be pretty bad if they're sending more than one crew.'

'It sounded quite serious,' Mary agreed worriedly. 'They think there may have been an escape of chlorine gas.'

'In that case we're going to need breathing apparatus.'

He strode to the door. 'Can you check if the local fire station has been alerted, Mary? We'll need their help to get the people out of the building. And can you let everyone know that we'll be unavailable for some time? All appointments and house calls will have to wait while we deal with this.'

'Will do,' the receptionist agreed, hurrying away as he turned to Francesca.

'We'd better both go out to this. If there's an unknown number of casualties, we can't risk just one of us going and not being able to cope.'

'Of course,' she agreed immediately. 'Is there anything I should take with me?'

'Just the usual,' he replied, steeling himself when she joined him by the door and he inhaled the fragrance of her perfume, something warm and spicy that made his head swirl dangerously. It was only the fact that they could be facing a very difficult situation that kept him focused, in fact.

'Hopefully, most of the casualties will be suffering from minor lung and eye irritation but there's bound to be some whose breathing has been compromised,' he continued as they left the staff room. 'They're going to need support until the ambulances arrive.'

'We'll be taking oxygen with us?' she queried, keeping pace with him as they hurried along the corridor.

'Yes. I'll get that all sorted out.' He paused outside the storeroom. 'I suggest that we each take our own car. In the event that one of us isn't needed, we'll be able to come back here and attend to our own patients.'

'Fine. I'll meet you in the car park.'

She didn't waste time asking any more questions and hurried away. Alex quickly gathered together what they needed, adding to the growing pile thermo-blankets and saline fluid to wash the chemical residue out of the casualties' eyes. It took several trips to ferry everything out to his car and Mary ran after him as he was loading the last lot into the back.

'Ambulance Control has just confirmed that the fire brigade is at the leisure centre. They've got breathing apparatus with them and they're bringing everyone out.'

'Good. That's one problem solved.' He slammed the car door and climbed into the driver's seat. Francesca was stowing her equipment into the boot of her car so he wound down his window.

'We're heading towards Beesley in case we get split up. There's bound to be a lot of traffic on the road once news of the incident spreads. The fire crews are on scene and the police should be there by now as well. You'll see a sign for the leisure centre on your right just before you reach the town so follow that.'

'Will do.'

She got into her car and started the engine. Alex led the way out of the car park, picking up speed once they'd left the village. He glanced in his rear-view mirror and smiled when she waved to him. He waved back, rather taken with the idea that she was happy to follow where he led. Maybe he was making a breakthrough at last?

He sighed. And maybe she was just eager to get on with the job!

Fran parked her car and lifted her case out of the boot. As Alex had predicted, they'd got split up on the way so she'd been glad of his directions. She spotted him talking to one of the firemen and headed towards him, weaving her way through the crowd that had gathered in the car park.

'So how many casualties are we talking about?' Alex was asking when she reached them.

'About forty,' the fireman replied.

'Forty!' Alex exclaimed.

Fran's heart sank because dealing with forty casualties was going to be a Herculean task for just the two of them.

'Yes, and the majority of them are kids, too.' The fireman pointed to a coach that was parked in the forecourt. 'The local junior school sends its year-five class to the baths every Tuesday. They'd just started their swimming lesson when the gas began leaking. The leisure centre staff managed to get most of them out but there were about half a dozen kids still inside the building when we arrived, plus five or six adults as well.'

'The kids who suffered the least exposure to the gas are on the bus and the rest are round the back in one of the Portakabins. We're just doing a final sweep of the building to check there's nobody else inside.'

'So that means there's at least a dozen casualties suffering from severe gas inhalation,' Alex clarified. 'Plus another couple of dozen or so who aren't as badly injured.'

'That's about right,' the fireman agreed.

Fran took a deep breath as the fireman hurried away because it was obvious they had a major incident on their hands. She turned to Alex, hoping he couldn't tell how nervous she felt. She'd never been involved in an incident on this scale before and could only hope she acquitted herself well.

'Shall I check the children on the bus while you take a look at the others? We need to decide who's in most urgent need of treatment, don't we?'

'Yes, that's our number one priority,' he agreed, and she felt some of her confidence come flooding back because she'd judged the situation correctly.

'What is the best way to handle it?' she asked because it would be foolish not to ask him for guidance.

'The immediate effects of exposure to chlorine gas are acute inflammation of the conjunctivae, nose, pharynx, larynx, trachea and bronchi so all the kids will be pretty distressed,' he explained. 'I've got saline in my car to wash out their eyes and there's also oxygen and a stack of space blankets. Some of them will be very shocked so it's a question of keeping them warm and reassuring them—the usual basic procedures.'

'And once I've finished checking them over, shall I send them back to school?'

'No, they'll need to be monitored for at least twenty-four hours because of the danger of pulmonary oedema. A child's tolerance for toxic gas is far less than an adult's and we can't take any chances. Send them straight to hospital once you've finished examining them. Just ask the coach driver to take them there.'

'It's going to put the A and E department under a lot of pressure if they have to deal with such a vast number of casualties,' she pointed out, and he sighed.

'It is but there's nothing we can do about that. Hopefully, most of the kids will be in A and E for only a short time. They'll be moved to the observation ward once they've been examined. I'm erring on the side of extreme caution so some of them may even be allowed to go home if their parents are happy to monitor them.'

'Fingers crossed the majority of the parents will opt to do that,' she said wryly. 'Anyway, I'll get them sorted out then come and find you.'

She ran over to his car and took what she needed then made her way to the coach and introduced herself to the teacher in charge. The poor woman was coughing hard and was obviously in some distress but she refused Fran's offer of assistance.

'No, no, I'm fine. Look after the children. They're more important than me.'

'Very well, but you must promise to see a doctor when you get to the hospital,' Fran told her firmly, making her way onto the bus. The children already had space blankets over their bathing costumes so she put the bundle she'd brought with her on the floor and went to the first row of seats where two little girls were sitting.

'Hi, I'm Francesca and I'm a doctor. I just want to see how you are.'

'I want my mummy,' one little girl told her, her lower lip wobbling.

'I know you do, poppet, and you'll be able to see her very soon.' She took her stethoscope out of her case and smiled at the child. 'Now, can you be a really brave girl and try not to cry while I listen to your chest?'

'I'll try.'

The little girl took a shuddering breath then sat very still while Fran examined her. She wasn't coughing and her chest sounded clear enough so she moved on to the other child. She, too, seemed to be breathing without any difficulty and her eyes weren't watering either. Fran's spirits rose because maybe the situation wasn't as dire as they'd feared.

'Zoë and Alice were still getting changed when the gas started to escape so they didn't breathe in the fumes like some of the others did,' the teacher told her as they crossed the aisle to where two little boys were sitting.

'That explains why they aren't coughing,' she said ruefully, bending down to introduce herself.

One of the boys was having problems with his eyes so she made him lie down on the seat while she washed away the chemicals with some saline. The other boy was coughing so she fetched the oxygen and popped a mask on him then made her way to the next row of seats. In the end there were just three children she wasn't entirely happy with so she told the teacher to make sure they were seen first when they reached the hospital and went to find Alex. The leisure centre was in the process of being renovated and one of the cabins normally used by the workmen had been turned into a temporary hospital bay. Alex was kneeling on the floor by the door when she arrived, working on a little boy who was having problems breathing. He looked up when she went in and she could see the concern in his eyes.

'He's really struggling. Can you bag him while I check his vital signs?'

'Is it just his airway that's affected?' she asked, kneeling down so she could take over the task of delivering oxygen to the child's lungs by means of an inflatable bag and pump device.

'So far, yes, but there's a very strong chance of pulmonary oedema setting in.' He checked the boy's blood pressure. 'He's inhaled a lot of gas and he's going to need specialist treatment. The sooner we get him to hospital the happier I'll be.'

'What about the others?' she asked, glancing around the cabin. There were a number of children lying on the floor and several of them were coughing quite badly, too. 'Are any of them as bad as this little fellow?'

'There's a couple I'm not happy with.' He nodded towards two little girls who were being cared for by some of the leisure centre staff. 'They're not as bad as he is but they were among the last to be brought out so they'll have inhaled a lot of gas.'

'It should never have happened!' she declared fiercely. 'There should have been safeguards in place to prevent an accident like this happening.'

'There are. However, the swimming pool has just been overhauled and a brand-new filtration system was installed. They're not sure what's gone wrong with it because they're waiting for the engineer to get here, but they think it might be a manufacturing fault.'

'Oh, I see.' She grimaced. 'Maybe I was a bit quick off the mark to lay the blame on the staff.'

'Don't apologise because you care, Fran.'

His voice echoed with something that sent a ripple scudding through her and Fran hurriedly returned her attention to the child, wishing that she'd been more careful. It made her feel extremely vulnerable to have allowed him that glimpse of her emotions and it was the last thing she needed at the moment.

They worked in silence while they waited for the ambulances. Alex got up several times to check on the other children, leaving her to carry on coaxing oxygen into the little boy's lungs. His BP and pulse had stabilised and although his breathing hadn't improved, it didn't seem to be getting any worse. Nevertheless, she was relieved when the ambulances started to arrive.

She handed the child over to the paramedics and started to clear up. The rest of the casualties were being loaded into the ambulances so it looked as though their part in the proceedings was over. She was just about to leave the Portakabin when a fireman came to find her.

'We've just found one of the workmen, Doc. He's in a really bad way so can you take a look at him?'

'Of course.' She grabbed hold of her case and followed him out of the cabin. 'Is he still inside the building?'

'Yes. It looks as though he was overcome by fumes and fell off some scaffolding. He's unconscious and we don't want to move him until we know if it's safe to do so.'

'What's going on?' Alex had been helping to load the casualties into the ambulances and now he came hurrying over to her.

'They've found a workman inside the building,' she explained. 'He's fallen off some scaffolding and they don't want to move him until they're sure it's safe to do so.'

'I'll come with you,' he offered immediately.

The fireman led them to the front of the building where the decontamination unit had been set up. 'The gas has almost cleared now but it's not worth taking any chances.

There's bound to be some residue about so you'll need to wear protective clothing as well as breathing apparatus. Have either of you used it before?'

'I have,' Alex replied. 'I'm part of the major incident team for this region so I've been trained to use all the apparatus.'

'Good. How about you, miss?'

'No. I've never had occasion to use it before,' she admitted. 'Is that going to be a problem?'

'Not so long as you do what I tell you to do,' the man assured her. 'Let's get you kitted up.'

Fran followed him into the decontamination unit where there were rows of protective suits hanging up. She took the one that was handed to her and put it on then let the fireman help her with the breathing apparatus. Alex was getting ready as well although he needed less assistance than she did because he'd done this before.

'Just breathe normally,' the fireman told her, checking the dials on the oxygen tank. 'You have plenty of oxygen so there's no need to worry about it running out.'

She breathed in and out a couple of times, trying to adjust to the feel of the mask covering her face. She felt very claustrophobic and she could only hope that she wouldn't disgrace herself by panicking.

'You'll be fine, Fran, so don't worry.'

She looked round when Alex appeared at her side, feeling some of her fear ease when he gave her a thumbs-up sign. He ushered her ahead of him as the fireman led them from the decontamination unit and it was reassuring to know that he was right behind her when they entered the building. Maybe it was crazy to feel like this but she felt safer, knowing he was there.

They made their way down some steps to the basement where the workman had ended up after he'd fallen off the scaffolding. Alex knelt down beside him and started to check his vital signs while she checked him for injuries. The fire crew had already fitted him with an oxygen mask but she could tell that his breathing was still very laboured, although whether that was a result of the gas he'd inhaled or an injury he'd sustained during the fall it was difficult to tell.

'BP is way down and his pulse is very thready, too,' Alex announced, his voice muffled by his face mask.

'His breathing isn't good either.' She took off her glove and slid her hand under the man's back so she could check his spine. 'I can't find anything obviously wrong with his spine,' she announced, putting her glove back on.

'And I can't see any sign of fractures to the limbs.' He frowned. 'There might be internal bleeding...possibly caused by damage to the pelvis. He could easily have fractured his pelvis in a fall like that although I can't feel any signs of instability,' he added, gently rotating the man's hips.

'There could be soft tissue damage, too. A ruptured spleen causes massive internal bleeding,' she pointed out, and he grimaced.

'Let's hope it isn't that or he might not survive the trip to hospital. Let's get him out of here and take another look to see if we can come up with anything else.'

He called the fireman over and told him they needed a spinal board. Fran fitted the man with a cervical collar and as soon as the stretcher arrived the firemen moved him onto it and carried him up the stairs.

'Take him straight to the Portakabin,' Alex instructed, ripping off his oxygen mask.

Fran followed him into the decontamination unit where they were helped out of their protective clothing before they hurried back to the cabin. The workman's condition had deteriorated and he was having serious problems breathing now, even with the oxygen. Alex frowned as they knelt down beside him.

'It could be pulmonary oedema caused by inhalation of the gas but it just doesn't feel right to me.'

He took his stethoscope out of his bag and listened to the man's chest. 'There's no crackling coming from his lungs to indicate they are full of fluid.' He draped the stethoscope round his neck and checked the man's airway again. 'No visible swelling either to indicate the oxygen isn't getting through.'

'So what do you think is wrong with him?' she asked worriedly.

'I'm not sure…' He hesitated then reached for his bag. 'It could be a haemothorax. If he's broken a rib, it could have punctured the lining of the chest wall. If his lungs are being compressed by a build-up of blood in the pleural cavity, that would explain the difficulty he's having breathing. It's worth checking it out.'

He took a wide-bore syringe out of his case as Fran quickly unbuttoned the man's shirt and grabbed an antiseptic wipe. He pointed to a spot on the side of the man's chest just below his arm.

'Just there… I need to go in between the ribs.'

She swabbed the area then watched as he slid the needle into the intercostal muscle. It was difficult to get it through the tough tissue but he finally succeeded. He pulled back the plunger and she gasped when she saw the bloodstained fluid that gushed into the syringe.

'You were right! It was a haemothorax.'

'Looks like it, although it doesn't mean he hasn't suffered any damage to his lungs from gas inhalation, of course.'

He removed the full syringe and repeated the procedure, this time inserting a cannula which he attached to a length of tubing. The end of the tube led into a sealed bottle which would collect the blood.

'Maybe not but he's breathing a lot better now,' she assured him, checking the man's condition once more. She taped the tube into place then looked round when someone came into the cabin. 'Aha, the cavalry has arrived again!'

He laughed as he turned to greet the paramedics. 'Another customer for you guys.'

The workman was quickly loaded into the ambulance and dispatched to hospital. Alex sighed as they watched it driving away. 'That's just about it. It's been quite a day, hasn't it?'

'It certainly has.' She grimaced. 'I wouldn't want to go through a repeat in a hurry, would you?'

'No. I wouldn't. Still, look on the bright side—it's been an experience, hasn't it?' He grinned at her and she laughed.

'Something to put in our CVs, you mean?'

'Something like that, although I'm hoping you won't need to update your CV in the forseeable future, Francesca. Now that I've found you, I really don't want to have to let you go.'

'I'm not thinking of leaving at the moment,' she said briskly, turning away because she certainly wasn't going to make the mistake of reading anything into that comment. He'd meant simply that he didn't want to lose her from the practice. After all, he'd admitted at her interview that he'd had problems finding someone suitable for the job so it was only natural that he should want her to stay in Teedale for as long as possible…

And that was all it was? a small voice whispered. She was absolutely certain that he didn't want her to stay here for any other reason?

She bit her lip because she didn't want to have to consider that idea. She had to think of Alex strictly as a colleague and couldn't afford to wonder if he viewed her in a different light. She tried to block the idea out of her mind as they made their way round to the front of the building. News of the incident had obviously spread because the car park was packed with sightseers now. There was even a team of reporters from one of the local television stations.

Fran shook her head when one of the reporters pushed a microphone into her face and demanded to know how many people had been injured. She'd had enough experience with the press after Paul had run out on her. Several of the tabloids had printed the story and even though she'd refused to answer their questions, it hadn't stopped them mentioning her name. It was a relief when Alex stepped in and rescued her.

'Sorry to hustle you about like that,' he said when they finally made it back to their cars. 'But if we'd got caught up in that scrum, we could have ended up stuck here for hours.'

'It's bedlam, isn't it?' she agreed as calmly as she could. She shot him a wary look but he seemed more concerned about the delay than anything else so she took her car keys out of her pocket, determined not to let him see that she was rattled by what had happened. 'It will be a relief to get back to the surgery.'

He laughed wryly. 'You won't be saying that when folk start grumbling about us missing their appointments!'

'Probably not,' she conceded. 'So what's the plan now? There's a stack of house calls that need doing and it's my turn, isn't it?'

'I think I'd better do them. It makes more sense because I know the area and can get round faster than you can.'

'I'll have to find my way around at some point.'

'Of course, but we're already way behind today and there's no point making the situation any worse, is there?' He glanced at his watch and groaned. 'It'll be touch and go whether I'll be back in time for evening surgery as it is.'

'I'll make a start on your list if you're not back,' she offered, not wanting him to think she was being difficult.

'That would be great. Thanks.' He went to his car and unlocked the door. 'I'll phone Mary and ask her for a list of calls to save me going all the way back to the surgery. I can update the patients' notes when I get back.'

'If you have any problems, ring me,' she told him, sliding behind the wheel.

'Will do.' He got into his car then paused. 'Damn! We never managed to sort out those rotas. We won't have time to do it this afternoon and tomorrow's out because I have to go into Ashbourne in the afternoon. There's a meeting of the primary health care trust—something to do with budgets, so I daren't miss it.' He sighed. 'I really wanted to get things organised so we both know what we're doing.'

'Could we get together tonight after surgery?' she suggested.

'That would be great, if you're sure you don't mind. It would need to be at my house, though, because of Daniel. Would that be a problem?'

'No...that will be fine,' she said quickly because she didn't want him to think that she was worried about spending the evening at his home.

'Excellent! It's a weight off my mind, I can tell you.' He started the engine and smiled at her. 'Let's make it seven-thirty, shall we? That will give me time to get Daniel to bed and have a quick tidy up.' He rolled his eyes. 'How one small boy can make so much mess is beyond me!'

'Seven-thirty is fine,' she assured him before she was tempted to change her mind.

She started her car, waving when Alex beeped his horn as he drove away. It didn't take her long to drive back to the surgery where she found a harried Mary holding the fort. Several people who'd had appointments to see her about their test results had decided to wait so she dealt with them first then phoned the rest and made her apologies before passing on the results.

Thinking about test results reminded her about Peter Arkwright, one of the patients she'd seen when she'd covered for Alex on the day of her interview. Alex hadn't mentioned what Peter Arkwright's test results had shown so she brought up the file onto the computer to see what the lab had found. There was no mention of any test results so she checked back and discovered that Peter had failed to turn up for his appointment. She sighed as she cleared the screen because it was annoying when a patient didn't show up for a test.

She worked steadily after that, seeing several of Alex's patients as well as her own before Mary informed her that he'd returned from doing the house calls. That lightened her load but it was gone six before she finished and Alex was still working, she noticed when she passed his room.

She took her files to the office and bade Mary goodnight then went back to the cottage, huffing out a sigh as she let herself in. It had been a busy day and it wasn't over yet. She still had to see Alex and sort out those rosters…

Her heart jerked so hard that she clutched her chest. She'd managed to control her apprehension while she'd been working but it was impossible to pretend that she didn't feel nervous about spending the evening with him. She would never have suggested it if she'd realised they would have to meet at his house. If there'd been a way to cry off, she would have done so, but backing out now would only give rise to questions so an hour later she was standing on his doorstep. She rang the bell, steeling herself not to betray any hint of the turmoil she was feeling when he opened the door.

'Hi! Come along in.'

Fran summoned a smile as she stepped into the hall. 'I hope I'm not too early?'

'No, you're bang on time.' He led the way to the sitting room and ushered her inside. 'I've managed to tidy up the worst of the mess in here so make yourself comfortable. I just need to finish reading Daniel's bedtime story and I'll be right with you.'

'We can always do this another time,' she suggested, hoping he couldn't tell how eager she was to make her escape. Maybe she was getting this out of proportion but she would much prefer to sort out the rotas during working hours. She needed to restrict her dealings with Alex and not start blurring the edges between social and professional.

'Of course not! I can't have you trailing backwards and forwards just because I can't get my act together.'

He put his hands on her shoulders and gently propelled her towards the sofa. 'It will only take a few minutes to settle him down—ten at the most—so pour yourself a glass of wine and relax. That's an order!'

With that he disappeared down the hall and a moment later she heard him running upstairs. She sat down on the sofa then immediately got up again and moved to a chair because she didn't want it to appear as though she expected him to sit next to her. There was an open bottle of wine and two glasses on the coffee-table but she made no attempt to help herself. She needed to keep a clear head and not cloud it with alcohol.

True to his word, Alex returned within a very short space of time. He frowned when he saw the empty wineglasses.

'You should have poured yourself a drink,' he admonished, filling the glasses before she had a chance to explain that she didn't want anything to drink.

'Thank you.' Fran took a token sip of the wine then set her glass on a coaster, but he shook his head.

'No, don't put your glass down just yet. I'd like to propose a toast first.' He held his glass aloft. 'To us, Francesca, and our new partnership. May we work together in harmony for many years to come.'

CHAPTER SEVEN

ALEX could sense Francesca's reluctance as she picked up her glass and couldn't help feeling hurt by it. She was so set on maintaining her distance that even drinking a toast to their partnership went against the grain. He had hoped that her attitude might have softened after the way they'd worked so well together at the leisure centre but nothing had changed. She was determined to set limits on their dealings with one another and he had to accept that.

'Thanks for picking up some of my appointments tonight,' he said, swallowing his frustration because it was fruitless wishing for something he couldn't have. 'It meant I could finish at a fairly reasonable time for once. I can't count the number of times I've ended up working way into the evening to get through all the appointments.'

'It wasn't a problem,' she said politely, unzipping her bag. She took out a notebook and looked enquiringly at him.

Alex's mouth tightened as he got up because it was obviously a hint that she wanted to get the meeting over as quickly as possible. He went to the bureau and took out a printed sheet listing all the clinics they held each month, trying not to let her unbending attitude get him down.

'I thought we could divide up the month between us.' He handed her the list and sat down. 'We also need to set up a rota for dealing with any calls outside surgery hours.'

'What do you suggest?'

'I'm easy, really.' He shrugged, hoping she couldn't tell how difficult it was for him to remain as detached as she appeared to be. Maybe she'd had more practice at it than him but he found it distressing to have to constantly guard against any warmth creeping in.

'We can work set nights each week or do turn and turn about if you prefer. Set nights are easier because then we'll always know who's supposed to be working, but it could be a bit restrictive if you wanted to go anywhere. You might want to spend an evening in London, for instance,' he clarified when she looked at him.

'As I'm not planning on spending my time anywhere except here at the moment, that really isn't an issue. Set nights would suit me best, too.'

'That's fine, then.'

He took a deep breath but he was going to have to say something if she kept this up. There was maintaining one's distance and going completely overboard, and she was definitely veering towards the latter. He summoned a smile, trying not to let her provoke him to say something he might regret.

'How about if I cover every Monday, Wednesday and Friday? Then you can do Tuesday, Thursday and Saturday, and we'll work alternate Sundays.'

'I'm happy with that so long as you are.'

'Good. That was easily sorted out, wasn't it?' he said with false bonhomie. He took a sip of his wine then cradled the glass in his hands as he looked steadily at her. 'Of course, there might be times when one of us wants a weekend off so we can negotiate them as and when it's necessary. Is that all right with you? Say if it isn't.'

'No, I don't have a problem with that. If you want a weekend off then just tell me and I'll be more than happy to cover for you.'

'Excellent! And it goes without saying that I'll do the same for you. If you need time off to see your family or friends, Francesca, just let me know.'

'Thank you.'

She inclined her head then looked studiously at the list again and he sighed. He hadn't consciously been probing for information, although it would have been nice if she'd opened up a bit.

He frowned when it struck him just how little he knew about her. Did she have any family, for instance: brothers, sisters, parents, cousins? She must have friends but surely they'd be living in London and she'd already said that she had no intention of going back there in the foreseeable future. The thought that she might be alone in the world was too hard to take so he ditched his good intentions about not asking any questions unrelated to work. Nobody could exist in a vacuum—as she seemed to want to do.

'Maybe we should work out a rota now for taking weekends off? After all, your family will want to know when you can visit them.'

'My parents emigrated to Barbados last year so it's not really practical to visit them for the weekend,' she explained, her eyes still glued to the list.

'Barbados? Now, that's somewhere I've always wanted to visit. Is it as beautiful as I imagine it to be?' he asked, trying not to sound too eager as he kept the conversational ball rolling in case she took fright.

'I really wouldn't know. I haven't been there.'

She glanced up and his heart contracted when he saw the bleakness in her eyes. It was all he could do not to reach out and squeeze her hand, only he knew how she would react if he did that.

'Something to look forward to,' he said heartily, hating to hear the falseness in his voice. The thought that she might be estranged from her family was a painful one but unless she was willing to tell him more about the situation, there was little he could do to help.

'Indeed. So how do you want to organise these clinics?

Are we going to share them between us or do you have a special interest in any of them?'

'The asthma clinic always tended to be my pet project when Trish and I were in practice together.' Alex took his cue from her and changed the subject. 'Trish was always more keen on the mother and baby clinic, although that doesn't mean we have to adopt the same routine, of course. Most of the clinics are held on a fortnightly basis so we could work them a month at a time. That way you'd get a better idea who the patients are than if you saw them only once every couple of months.'

'I'm happy with that. Maybe we could start tomorrow with me taking the antenatal clinic?' she suggested, pencil poised over her notebook.

'That would be perfect. I've got that meeting in Ashbourne tomorrow afternoon so it would make sense if you took the clinic. I'll cover the baby clinic on Thursday while you do any house calls then you can have the asthma clinic on Friday.'

'Sure you don't want to hold onto that one if it's of special interest to you? I don't mind doing the house calls two days on the run.'

'Well...' He wavered and her face softened into a sudden smile.

'I think that's a yes, don't you?'

'Only if you're sure you don't mind,' he agreed ruefully.

'Of course I don't mind. Anyway, you're the senior partner, Alex, so it isn't up to me to object.'

'I disagree.' He frowned. 'Your input into this practice is every bit as important as mine, Francesca. If you're not happy with the way things are done then you must say so. I don't want you to feel that you have to kow-tow to me because you're worried about losing your job.'

'I don't.'

'No?' He looked at her levelly. 'When you came for your

interview I got the impression that you were watching what you said. To be honest, it surprised me because you didn't strike me as someone who was lacking in confidence yet you seemed to be holding back all the time in case you said the wrong thing.'

'I imagine most people try to make a good impression at an interview,' she countered but he saw the colour rush up her face and knew that he was right. Maybe it was that which made him decide to press home the advantage.

'I expect they do, but it was more than that with you. You really wanted this job and it puzzles me why you were so keen to get it.'

He shrugged, watching her closely so that he saw her eyelids flutter in panic. Even though it didn't make him feel good to know he was upsetting her, he was determined to get to the bottom of this mystery. 'Why, Francesca? Why were you so eager to get out of London that you threw up a job with excellent prospects and moved here?'

'As I've told you already, I needed to make some changes to my life and what better way to do it than to move to a completely different part of the country?'

She stood up, making it clear that she wasn't willing to answer any more questions, but he refused to give up that easily.

'It still seems a very drastic decision to have made. You've completely altered your life and people don't do that unless they have a very strong incentive. It makes me wonder if you were running away from something...'

'That's ridiculous!'

'Or someone.'

The words hung in the air and he saw her blanch as she gripped the back of the chair. Alex stood up, wondering if he'd gone too far, and yet he knew that he wouldn't rest until he'd got at the truth.

'Am I right, Fran? Were you running away?'

Tears suddenly welled to her eyes and she turned her head away. 'It has nothing to do with you,' she said, her voice catching.

'Maybe not but I'd still like to know what happened.'

'So you can give me some good advice?' She laughed harshly and his heart spasmed when he heard the bitterness in her voice. 'No, thank you. I had my fill of advice the same as I had my fill of sympathy so I'll pass on your offer!'

'I have no intention of offering you any advice. I just want to help if I can.'

'Why? What's in it for you, Alex?' She tossed back her head and glared at him. 'Will it make you feel superior to know that I allowed myself to be conned? Or are you worried in case something in my past might reflect badly on you and your practice? That's what happened in my last job, of course: the senior partners were worried in case all the publicity ruined their reputation. Maybe they were right, too, and you should be worried!'

'I have no idea what you're talking about,' he ground out, his head reeling as he tried to make sense of what she was telling him. He put out his hand and stopped her when she attempted to leave. 'No. You can't go without explaining what you just said. What do you mean about being conned, and what did it have to do with your former employers? I'm sorry, Francesca, but I need to know what's been going on.'

Fran took a deep breath but the panic that had her in its grip refused to die down. She wished with all her heart that she hadn't said anything but wishing wasn't going to undo the damage now. Shrugging off his hand, she sat down again on the chair and after a second Alex resumed his own seat. He leant forward and she could see the concern in his eyes as he studied her.

'Tell me what happened, Francesca. Please.'

It was the 'please' that did it, one small word which unlocked the door so that the words came tumbling out. She knew she could be making a huge mistake by telling him what had happened but she could no longer keep it to herself. It was important that he knew the truth—for many reasons.

Her heart hiccuped at that thought but she blanked it out because she couldn't deal with it now. 'I should have told you at my interview. It would have been fairer to let you know about the publicity if nothing else.'

'What kind of publicity are we talking about?' he asked calmly, and for some reason that helped to steady her.

'I was caught up in all the publicity when my fiancé went bankrupt. A lot of people lost an awful lot of money when Paul's firm went bust and the papers made a lot of the scandal.'

'And were you involved in what happened? Apart from your involvement with your fiancé, I mean?'

She shook her head. 'No. I had no idea what was going on. It was as much of a surprise to me as it was to everyone else. In fact, I lost a lot of money, too, but the papers omitted any mention of that fact.'

'You'd invested in the firm?' His brows rose steeply and she bit her lip because this was the worst part of the tale, to her mind, the part that showed her in the worst possible light.

'I invested all the money from a trust fund my grandparents had set up for me when I was born as well as my savings.' She took a quick breath but she may as well get everything out into the open in one go rather than hold anything back. 'I also remortgaged my flat and gave the proceeds to Paul to help him through what he termed a ''difficult patch''. Suffice to say that I lost every penny of that as well.'

'But why on earth did he take so much money off you if there was a chance he'd lose it? Surely there must have been other ways of financing his business—banks, loans…'

'But they would have required proof of the business's viability and that was the one thing Paul couldn't have given them.' She gave a sad little laugh. 'You see, there was no business. Paul had spent all the money people had invested on his gambling debts. He must have gambled away millions of pounds and nobody had any idea, least of all me.'

'It's incredible! You mean, he *invented* a business so he could con folk out of money?'

'Yes. That's the top and the bottom of it. He told everyone he was a fund manager with his own investment firm in the City. Oh, he had an office there, all right, but he never traded on the stock market or made any investments. He also claimed that he was affiliated to another well-known firm which has offices in London but they'd never heard of him. It was one of their clients, in fact, who raised the alarm. Paul met this man at a party and offered to invest some money for him. The man decided to check up on him first but when he phoned the company he usually dealt with they told him that they'd never heard of Paul Bryant Investments and that he most certainly wasn't affiliated to them. All hell broke out after that.'

'And you had no idea... Of course you didn't,' he said brusquely, answering his own question.

Fran smiled gratefully. 'Thank you for that vote of confidence. I wish more people had felt that way. Sadly, a lot of folk believed I was party to his scheme, hence all the bad publicity.'

'It must have been a nightmare for you.' His eyes darkened as he leant over and squeezed her hands. 'To find out like that... Well, what can I say?'

'It was awful,' she admitted hollowly. 'Paul had taken money off so many people, even our friends, and it caused a lot of bad feeling. Some folk were very supportive but there were a lot of people who thought I'd been working with him and was guilty of conning investors out of their savings.'

'Mud sticks to everyone, unfortunately, not just to the guilty. You said that the senior partners in your last practice were unhappy about what had happened.'

'Yes. I could understand why, too, because the surgery was bombarded with phone calls from journalists. They were even hanging around outside and pestering our patients. In the end, I decided that the best thing I could do was to leave and find a job well away from all the furore.'

'And that's why you came here?' He nodded. 'It makes sense and it was probably the best thing for you. You needed to get away...'

He stopped and she frowned.

'What?'

'I'm assuming that you left your fiancé,' he said carefully. 'You haven't actually said what happened between you and him.'

'I never got the chance to leave him. As soon as the news broke, Paul disappeared. I got home that night and discovered that he'd packed all his belongings and gone. I don't know where he went—probably abroad—Spain or France, perhaps—but the police never managed to trace him.'

'So you've not spoken to him since?'

'No, and I don't want to speak to him either. He played me for a fool and I'll never forgive him for what he did!'

Tears suddenly overwhelmed her and she heard Alex sigh as he got up and came over to her. He took her gently in his arms, rocking her to and fro until the worst of the storm abated. Plucking a tissue from the box on the coffee-table, he handed it to her and smiled.

'Here, mop up those tears and blow your nose. That's an order.'

'Thank you.'

She wiped her eyes then took a deep breath, because difficult though it was, she knew that she had to give him the option of terminating her contract. It wasn't fair to expect him to accept what she'd done without there being any consequences. Her voice shook because the thought of having to leave Teedale and Alex was so painful.

'I'll understand if you decide you don't want me to carry on working here, Alex. I should have told you the truth at my interview so there's no need to feel that you have to honour my contract.'

'Why on earth would I want you to leave?'

'Because, as you said, mud sticks and there's no knowing if the story might surface in the future.' She bit her lip because this was far more difficult than she'd expected it to be. 'I wouldn't want to cause problems for you so it might be best if I tender my resignation.'

'You can if you want to but I have to warn you that I won't accept it.' He smiled at her, his eyes so full of compassion that she almost burst into tears again. 'You didn't do anything wrong, Fran. You were duped by that... *sleazeball* the same way everyone else was.'

'But I should have realised what he was like! I work with people every day of my life so I should have been able to tell that he was stringing me along...'

'You were in love with him. It's only natural that you wouldn't have suspected what was happening.' His tone was flat all of a sudden and she frowned because she wasn't sure what he was thinking at that moment.

'I suppose so but I still feel stupid for letting myself be duped like that. My parents were furious when they found out. My mother told me that she was ashamed of me for what I'd done and that there was no way that she and father would bail me out because I'd got myself into such a mess. I...I haven't spoken to either of them since,' she added miserably.

'It wasn't your fault,' he said. 'You were a victim of a

cruel trickster. As for your parents, well, they'll come round once they get over the shock. Now the best thing you can do is to put what's happened behind you and get on with your life.'

'That's what I wanted to do but are you absolutely sure you still want me here, Alex?'

'Positive!' He smiled at her and it felt as though a weight had been lifted off her shoulders when she saw the certainty in his eyes.

'Thank you.'

'You won't be thanking me when you're stuck up the side of a hill in the middle of the night attending a house call,' he warned her with a grin, and she laughed.

'Probably not! But I'll remind myself that it's preferable to being in the middle of a pack of rabid reporters all trying to get a scoop.'

'That's better.' He laughed when she looked quizzically at him.

'Better?'

'Mmm. You're starting to look for the silver lining instead of only seeing the clouds. It's a step in the right direction, Fran.'

'It is, isn't it?' she said slowly then suddenly smiled. 'It definitely is!'

'So now that we both know you're going to stay, we need to make sure that you're up to speed with the job.'

'What do you mean?' she asked, bristling slightly because it had sounded like a bit of a slur on her capabilities.

'Working here is going to be very different from what you're used to. Just finding your way around is going to pose problems.'

'I have an Ordnance Survey map,' she pointed out rather sharply, and he sighed.

'I'm not doubting your orienteering capabilities, Francesca. It just makes sense to be sure you know where you're going before you start doing any calls at night. Finding your way around in the dark isn't easy, as I know to my cost. I got lost several times when I first came here and it's no fun being stuck in the middle of nowhere in the pitch dark.'

'I appreciate that so what do you suggest?' she asked more quietly.

'That we give you a thorough grounding in where everything is in relation to the village. I suggest we go out together this weekend so I can show you around. Once you've an idea where everything is, you should be fine.'

He held up his hand when she opened her mouth to protest that he didn't need to go to all that trouble. 'This is as much for our patients' benefit as yours, Fran. I can't take the risk of them phoning for assistance and nobody turning up. Their needs have to come first so we'll spend Saturday exploring, if that's all right with you.'

Frankly, Fran wasn't sure if it was a good idea. Even though they'd cleared up the most important issue, she knew it would be a mistake to get too involved with Alex. She was very vulnerable after what had happened with Paul and it would be silly to take any risks. However, it was obvious from his tone that he didn't intend to let her fob him off with any excuses.

'If you feel it's necessary then that's what we'll do.'

'I do.' He inclined his head but the gleam in his eyes told her that he'd noted her reluctance. 'We'll sort out the arrangements on Friday although we'll probably need to make an early start if we hope to cover everything in one trip.'

'Just let me know what time you want to meet me,' she said as evenly as she could. She stood up and held out her hand, wanting to put a little more distance between them again. 'Thank you for being so understanding. I'll make sure I don't let you down.'

'I'm quite sure you won't.'

He shook her hand then opened the sitting-room door. Fran led the way along the hall, pausing when she came to the front door. In her heart she knew how difficult it was going to be to maintain her distance now that she'd poured out the whole sorry story to him but she had to try because she couldn't afford to make another mistake.

'I'll see you in the morning, then. Thanks for the wine.'

'My pleasure.'

He didn't wait to wave her off but closed the door as soon as she'd moved off the step. Fran went back to the cottage and made straight for the kitchen. She put the kettle on for tea then took some eggs out of the fridge. An omelette would be quick to make and she needed to eat something because the wine was starting to make her feel giddy...

She took a deep breath because there was no point pretending the alcohol had gone to her head. She'd only had a couple of sips and if she felt dizzy it was because of what had happened. Alex had accepted what she'd told him far better than she could have hoped he would. He didn't seem to blame her for Paul's transgressions and didn't appear to believe it would affect her job at the surgery. She should have felt elated that things had turned out so well but she couldn't help worrying about the future.

She liked Alex a lot even though she'd tried not to feel anything for him. He was kind and considerate, and fun to be with, too. That he was also extremely good-looking in a craggy, unselfconscious way was another point in his favour but she really and truly didn't want to be so aware of all his good points. She'd nearly ruined her life once by falling for a man whom she'd thought was ideal and she could no longer rely on her own judgement. She knew from various friends' experiences how easy it was to leap from one bad situation into another for all the wrong reasons and she wasn't going to allow that to happen to her.

She took a deep breath. She would have to be very careful on Saturday and keep a tight rein on her emotions—even tighter than usual, in fact. Now that she understood Alex's attraction, she must be on her guard.

CHAPTER EIGHT

BY THE time Saturday arrived, Alex was having serious doubts about the wisdom of what he was doing. Granted his motives had been sound enough but he couldn't put his hand on his heart and swear that he'd been driven solely by a desire to improve Francesca's knowledge of the surrounding countryside. Spending time with her had also been high up on his agenda and it worried him after what she'd told him the other night.

She must be feeling very vulnerable after what had happened to her and he would never forgive himself if he took advantage of her susceptibility. Her ex-fiancé had done his best to ruin her life and it would take her a long time to get over an experience like that. It didn't matter if he was interested in getting to know her better because he had to put her needs first so he decided to use Daniel as a buffer. There was nothing like having a lively eight-year-old around to keep one's feet on the ground!

It was gone eight by the time he and Daniel were ready to set off. Alex bent and looked his son firmly in the eyes. 'Now, I want you to promise me that you'll be on your very best behaviour today. I need to show Francesca where everything is so that she won't get lost when she has to do any house calls.'

'OK, but we don't have to drive round *all* the time, do we, Dad?' Daniel pleaded. 'Can't we stop and have a game of football?'

'We'll see.' He ruffled his son's hair. 'If you're *really* good there might be time for one game.'

'Brill! I'll fetch my ball.'

He sighed as Daniel went thundering off down the hall because he had no idea how Francesca would feel about the promised treat. However, it seemed a bit mean to expect the child to sit quietly in the car all day long. He would just have to hope that she'd put up with half an hour's rough and tumble!

He'd arranged to pick her up at eight-thirty and it was exactly that when he drew up in front of the cottage. He beeped the horn and a moment later she appeared. Alex felt his heartbeat quicken as he watched her cross the pavement because it was the first time he'd seen her casually dressed. Like him, she'd opted for jeans that day and they made her legs look longer than ever. She'd teamed them with a white shirt and a pale grey cashmere pullover and the effect was simple yet classy. Tan leather boots on her feet and a navy blue, down-filled jacket to ward off the chill of the April morning completed her outfit. She looked so stunning, in fact, that by the time she opened the car door, he was having a hard time thinking straight, but, thankfully, Daniel wasn't suffering from his inhibitions.

'Can you play football?' the child demanded as soon as she slid into the passenger seat.

'Football?' she repeated, glancing uncertainly at him.

'I promised Daniel that I'd have a game of football with him if he was *really* good,' Alex explained huskily. He cleared his throat, determined not to appear a real idiot. 'I think he's checking if it's worth having you on his team.'

'Oh, right. I understand now.' She gave him a quick smile then turned to the child. 'I've never played football so it might be best if you counted me out.'

'Dad and I can show you what to do,' Daniel offered immediately, and Alex smiled to himself because it was typical of his son not to want to leave her out.

'Um… Right. Thank you.'

Francesca turned to face the front again and he could tell that she was a little nonplussed by the offer.

'Don't worry,' he told her as he started the engine. 'We'll treat you very gently because you're a complete beginner. We won't expect you to score too many goals, will we, Daniel?'

'No. You don't have to worry, Fran, 'cos we know that girls are *rubbish* at football,' Daniel assured her seriously.

Alex laughed as he pulled away from the kerb. 'He doesn't get his sexist attitude from me, I swear. I'm a firm believer in the equality of the sexes.'

'Even when it comes to sport?' she retorted sweetly.

'Well...'

She laughed and his heart put on an extra little spurt because he'd never heard her sounding so carefree before. 'I rest my case. So, leaving aside the thorny subject of who's best at football, what's the plan for the day?'

'I thought we'd do a tour of the town then work our way around the surrounding area. Teedale is roughly in the middle of our catchment area so that way you should get a better idea where everything is in relation to the village.'

Alex briskly returned his thoughts to the reason why they were spending the day together. He slowed the car and set about pointing out all the places she needed to know. Although she would have discovered many of them already, he wanted to be sure that she had an overall picture of the village before they went any further so he stopped when they came to the end of the main street.

'If you carry on along this road, you'll come to Ashbourne. And if you drive in the opposite direction you'll reach Beesley. I'm sure you know that but I just want to make certain that you have an idea in which direction everything lies.'

'I understand,' she agreed, glancing back the way they'd come. 'What if you leave the village via that road next to the post office? Where does it lead? I've not been that way yet.'

'Yes, you have.' He turned the car around and headed back to the centre of the village. 'We went this way the night we had to go to Marie Fisher's home to deliver her baby.'

'Oh! I didn't realise this was the route we took.' She nodded when they reached the crossroad and he turned left. 'Yes, I remember this bit, where the road runs alongside that old barn. How is Marie, by the way? And the baby? What did they call him?'

'Marie's fine and so is the baby. She had to stay in hospital for a few days but she's had no problems since she returned home. They called the baby George after Marie's father. He's absolutely thrilled about it, too.'

'That must be one of the best things about working in a practice like this,' she observed softly. 'You get to know your patients so well.'

'Didn't that happen at your last post?'

'Not really. Oh, there were a few people I got to know fairly well, but the population fluctuates so much in a city. People move in and out again within the space of a few months. And, of course, it's highly unlikely that you'll get to know their families because so many people living in London have moved there from other parts of the country.'

'I never thought about that. A migrant population must be very different to the kind of set-up we have here. Most people who live in Teedale were born here. There's very few outsiders apart from a couple of people who own holiday homes in the area and the tourists, of course.'

'It must make for better continuity of care.'

'From the cradle to the grave, you mean?' He laughed. 'It must seem very old-fashioned to you.'

'No. It feels *permanent* and that's something I really like about working here. Very little in life is permanent nowadays,' she added wistfully.

Alex knew what she was thinking about: her fiancé's defection had disrupted her whole life so it was little wonder that she found the idea of permanency so attractive. He only wished he could say something to make her feel better but there was little he could do to alleviate the heartache she must be suffering, and it hurt to know how powerless he was to help her.

In the end, he kept up a running commentary as they drove until he was hoarse from talking so much but it was better than letting himself get carried away by the idea that he could make her life any better. She wasn't interested in anything he had to offer apart from this job and it was a salutary reminder he had to heed. If he'd had a choice he would have treated her like the desirable woman she was, but she wouldn't welcome his advances after her recent experiences.

He groaned under his breath because he couldn't believe that he was falling for a woman who probably didn't care if he existed!

They stopped at noon for something to eat. Fran would have preferred it if they'd carried on so they could have got the day over as quickly as possible, but Daniel was growing increasingly restless and it didn't seem fair to object when Alex announced they would stop for lunch.

He turned into a gateway and switched off the engine. 'We'll stop here. This field is part of Peter Arkwright's land and I'm sure he won't mind if we eat our picnic here.'

'I meant to ask you about Peter Arkwright,' she said as Daniel bounded out of the car. 'Did you know that he never turned up for that blood test I ordered?'

'Didn't he?' Alex frowned as he slammed the door. 'Maybe he was feeling better so decided not to bother.

Farmers are their own worst enemies when it comes to their health. They hate taking time off work but you could ask Mary to follow it up if you're concerned.'

'I think I shall.'

She went round to the back of the car and waited while he opened the boot. He handed her a tartan rug then lifted out a picnic hamper and placed it by his feet.

'The ground could be a bit damp at this time of the year so we'll lay this old tarpaulin under the rug,' he explained, heaving a length of heavy canvas out of the back.

'D'you need a hand with that?' she offered, but he shook his head.

'No, I can manage, thanks. If you can bring the hamper and the rug, I'll carry this.'

Fran picked up the basket and followed him to the gate. There was a stile set to one side and Alex climbed over it first then turned to help her. She passed him the basket then climbed over, gasping when the heel of her boot caught on the top pole and she pitched forward.

'Careful!'

He caught her as she fell and she gasped again when she found herself suddenly crushed against his chest. She could feel the steady thud of his heart beneath her breasts and was overwhelmed by a sudden need to lay her head on his chest. The past, horrible year had sapped her strength and he felt so strong, so capable. She would have given anything to lean on him but she couldn't take the risk of getting used to having him take care of her.

'Are you all right?' he asked as she pulled away, and she shuddered when she heard the grating note in his voice. It was obvious that he'd been equally affected by her nearness and it was hard to behave as though nothing had happened.

'I'm fine,' she said primly and with a deliberate lack of warmth.

'Good.'

He gave her a tight smile then picked up the hamper and handed it to her. Fran didn't say anything as she followed him across the field. There wasn't anything she could say because if she apologised for rebuffing him, he'd want to know why she'd done it. How could she explain that she was afraid to get too close to him in case it wasn't what she really wanted?

'Goal!'

Daniel roared with delight as the ball shot past the sticks that marked the boundaries of the makeshift goal mouth and Fran grinned as she wiped her grubby hands down her equally grubby jeans. In an effort to dispel all the thoughts which had been crowding her head, she'd decided to join in the football match and had just succeeded in scoring her very first goal.

'Offside. That was definitely offside.'

She looked round when a disgruntled Alex came hurrying over to them. They'd split into teams: she and Daniel playing against Alex. Now she treated him to a haughty look.

'Just because the score happens to be three nil in our favour doesn't mean you can start objecting.'

'You were offside.' He put his hands on his hips. 'Anyone with twenty-twenty vision could see that.'

'Rubbish! I've no idea what "offside" means but you're just peeved because you're losing. Isn't that right, Daniel?'

'Yes. Don't be such a spoilsport, Dad. That was a brilliant goal and you know it was. You're just upset because Fran didn't want to be on your team!'

'OK, I know when I'm beaten. If the pair of you are going to gang up on me there's not much I can do.' He looked pained. 'We'll just have to settle this the next time we play. *Then* we'll see which is the better team.'

'We'll probably beat you again so then you'll just end up losing a second time,' Daniel piped up, laughing when Alex playfully attempted to cuff his ear. He picked up his football and dashed off towards the trees. Fran watched him go, an unconsciously tender smile curving her mouth. 'He's a great child, Alex. A real credit to you.'

'Thanks.'

There was a strained note in his voice and she looked at him in surprise. 'That was meant to be a compliment.'

'I know, and believe me it meant a lot to me, too.' He sighed. 'I'm very aware that I don't spend nearly enough time with him nowadays. It would have been different if Trish was here—we'd have shared everything between us. I always feel that Daniel got the short straw. Not only did he lose his mother, but his father is too busy to pay enough attention to him.'

'That's ridiculous! Anyone can see how much you love him and how much he loves you. Maybe you can't be with him every minute of the day but you do everything in your power to make sure he knows that he's loved and wanted, and that's more important than anything else.'

'Thanks.' He gave her a crooked smile that made her heart turn over when she saw the warmth it held. 'I think I was in danger of getting a little bit maudlin.'

'And we can't have that,' she said rousingly because it was upsetting to hear him blaming himself when there was no need.

She quickly made her way back to where they'd left the picnic basket because she couldn't afford to start worrying about Alex. She had to maintain her distance for his sake as well as her own. He'd suffered enough when his wife had died and it would be grossly unfair to encourage him when she wasn't in the market for another relationship. She packed away the hamper while he folded up the tarpaulin and they were just about to take everything back to the car when Daniel came rushing out of the woods.

'Dad, Dad, you've got to come! Quick!'

Alex dropped the tarpaulin and ran to his son. 'What's the matter?'

'Mr Arkwright is lying in the stream!' the child explained fearfully, his eyes as big as saucers. 'I tried talking to him but he didn't answer me.'

'I'll go and take a look at him.' Alex turned as she ran over to them and she could see the concern on his face as he drew her aside. 'Would you mind keeping Daniel here with you? I don't want him to go back there until I see how bad things really are.'

'Of course not. Just give me a shout if you need any help.'

'I shall. Thanks.'

Fran put her arm around the little boy as Alex ran into the woods. Daniel was obviously very frightened by what he'd seen because she could feel him trembling. 'There's no need to be scared,' she said gently. 'I'm sure your dad will sort everything out.'

'What if Mr Arkwright's dead?' His lower lip wobbled. 'Dad won't be able to make him better then, will he?'

'No, but he might just be ill,' she explained, mentally crossing her fingers.

'S'ppose so,' the child agreed slowly. 'I thought my pet hamster was dead once but he was just asleep. Maybe Mr Arkwright's asleep and he didn't hear me talking to him.'

'You could be right,' she agreed, pleased to hear that he sounded a lot less frightened.

They sat down on the rug and waited for Alex to come back. Fran would have dearly loved to go and see what was happening but she didn't want to leave Daniel on his own. When Alex appeared some ten minutes later, he was carrying Peter Arkwright over his shoulder.

'He's alive but he's in a pretty bad way,' he explained as she ran to meet him. 'He's suffering from hypothermia from the look of him so we need to get him back home and warm him up.'

'Back to the surgery, you mean?' she queried, following him across the field. Fortunately the gate wasn't padlocked and she managed to tug open the bolt to save him having to lift the farmer over the stile.

'No, back to his farm. It's just a mile or so from here and we don't want to waste time by driving all the way back to the village.'

He frowned as she opened the car door so he could lay the man along the back seat. 'We could do with getting him out of these wet clothes, though.'

'I'll fetch the rug. If we wrap him in that, it might help to warm him up.'

'Good idea. And fetch the tarpaulin as well. It will help to keep in the heat.' He quickly stripped off the man's jacket then started to unbutton his shirt.

'Here, use this.' She handed him her down jacket then ran back to where Daniel was still waiting. 'Mr Arkwright is very cold so we need to warm him up,' she explained. 'Can you take this rug to your dad while I fetch the tarpaulin?'

She handed the boy the rug then picked up the heavy canvas sheet and staggered back to the car with it. Alex took it off her with a murmur of thanks. He'd already wrapped Peter in the rug and her jacket and now he laid the tarpaulin over him as well. He'd also used his sweater as a makeshift hat—essential to conserve any remaining body heat.

'That's the best we can do for now,' he announced, slamming the door. Opening the tailgate, he unfolded the spare seat and helped Daniel buckle his safety belt before hurrying to the driver's side. 'We'll leave the rest of our things here and come back for them later.'

It took them just a few minutes to reach the farm where

they were met by a cacophony of barking as they drew up outside the farmhouse. Alex shooed the dogs out of the way as he got out of the car and turned to her.

'Can you and Daniel see if you can find anything to warm him up with? Hot-water bottles would be perfect. And if there's a room with a fire in it…'

'I'll sort it out,' she assured him, hurrying Daniel towards the house. Fortunately, the back door wasn't locked so she let them into the kitchen and sighed in relief when she saw the ancient old Aga because it immediately solved the problem of providing a source of heat.

'Can you see if you can find some hot-water bottles?' she asked Daniel. 'There might be some upstairs in the bedrooms so can you have a look? I'll just stoke up the fire to make sure it's nice and warm in here.'

The child went racing off while she unlatched the range door and added another shovel of coal to the blaze. There was a thick rag-rug on the floor in front of the stove and when Alex carried the man into the farmhouse, she pointed to it.

'Lay him down there while I fetch some blankets.'

She ran upstairs and stripped a couple of blankets off one of the beds. Daniel was coming along the landing and he grinned as he showed her two old-fashioned rubber hot-water bottles.

'Will these do?'

'They're perfect!' she declared, smiling at him.

They took everything back to the kitchen and Alex filled the hot-water bottles while she tucked the blankets around the farmer. His skin was starting to lose the characteristic waxy pallor that typified a severe drop in temperature and he felt warmer to the touch. She checked his pulse as well and was pleased to find that it was almost back to normal.

'How's he doing?'

Alex came back with the hot-water bottles which he'd

wrapped in towels. Fran took them off him and slid them under the blankets.

'Not too badly. His pulse is near enough normal now and he's starting to get a bit of colour back into his skin. How long do you think he was in the stream?'

'It's hard to say.'

He crouched down beside her and she bit her lip when his arm accidentally brushed hers and she felt a ripple of awareness shoot through her. 'Even in the height of summer, the water in British rivers is very cold and at this time of the year it's barely above freezing. You wouldn't need to be immersed for very long before your temperature dropped.'

'It's lucky that Daniel spotted him,' she said huskily, moving over to make some space between them.

'It is.' He stood up abruptly. 'I'll put the kettle on. Once Peter comes round, we'll give him a hot drink. That will help.'

Fran sighed as he moved away because it was obvious that he'd noticed her reaction and there was nothing she could do about it. She was already far more aware of him than she wanted to be and couldn't afford to let the situation develop. It wasn't easy to keep him at arm's length—because there was something about him that she responded to—but she had to do what was right for both of them. They could only ever be colleagues and it would be wrong to let him think they could be more than that.

Peter started to come round a few minutes later, looking groggy and disorientated when he saw them.

'What's happened? What are you doing here, Dr Shepherd?'

'We found you lying in the stream at the bottom of Dean Wood,' Alex explained, kneeling beside him. He checked Peter's pulse, taking care not to touch Francesca as he did so because it was hard enough to deal with the memory of how she'd shrunk away from him without risking a repeat. 'Do you know how you got there?'

'I'm not sure…' Peter frowned as he tried to piece it all together. 'I know I went out to look for one of the goats that had got out of its pen. And I remember heading towards the woods…' He shook his head. 'No, it's no good. I can't remember what happened after that. Mind you, I've not been feeling so good these past few days so maybe I passed out.'

'And ended up in the stream,' Alex concluded dryly. 'I don't know how long you were in the water but you're suffering from mild hypothermia. We need to bring your core temperature back to normal so you just lie there while I make you a cup of tea.'

'But I've got jobs to do,' Peter protested. 'I can't be lying around here when there's animals to tend to.'

'It's either that or hospital,' he said sternly. 'Which is to be?'

Peter conceded defeat, albeit with bad grace, so Alex made the tea. Francesca had fetched his case out of the car and once the farmer had drunk his tea, they checked him over. Apart from a nasty graze on his shin, Peter appeared to have got off remarkably lightly and Alex told him so.

'It could have been a lot worse. You said you hadn't been feeling well for a few days—in what way?'

'Just the old trouble,' Peter muttered, looking embarrassed. 'Kind of feverish and headachy…that sort of thing.'

'Exactly the same as when I saw you at the surgery,' Fran said blandly.

'Aye. Suppose so,' the man admitted grudgingly.

'Then don't you think it's time we found out what is wrong with you?' Alex said firmly. 'Dr Goodwin told me that you missed your appointment for a blood test so I'll call round on Monday morning and take a sample.'

'If you really think it's necessary, Dr Shepherd,' Peter conceded.

'I do. In fact, I'd say it's essential if we want to avoid a repetition of what happened today. In the meantime, we need to make sure that you don't go doing anything silly.'

He stood up. 'I'll give Jim Fisher a call and see if he can give you a hand with your animals. I'm also going to phone Hilary Johnson, our practice nurse, and ask her to spend the night here. At least I'll know you can't get up to any mischief with Hilary here!'

Peter looked glum although he didn't argue. Once everything was arranged they helped him to bed and left him there with strict instructions not to get up. Hilary arrived a short time later and promised to keep a stern eye on the patient once Alex had explained what had happened. They left her to it and went out to the car where Francesca paused to glance back.

'I hope Hilary can cope. Peter doesn't seem the easiest of patients so I hope we aren't expecting too much of her.'

He laughed as he ushered Daniel into the back seat. 'He won't get round Hilary. She's a stickler when it comes to following doctor's orders.'

'Good.' She smiled as she got into the car. 'Peter needs someone to take him in hand. Does he live here on his own?'

'Yes. Someone told me that his father was a bit of a tartar and kept him on a very tight rein when he was a young man so he never married. Old Mr Arkwright died last year so Peter's been here on his own ever since. Mr Arkwright was in his eighties but he could do the work of a man half his age and I imagine Peter must be finding it difficult to cope.'

'Can't he employ someone to help him?' she suggested, and he sighed when he realised that the chill was creeping back into her voice. He knew that she was deliberately raising those barriers again and it was frustrating not to be able to do anything about it. All he could do was hope that she would learn to trust him in time, although there was no guarantee after what had happened.

It was a depressing thought but he did his best not to let his feelings show as he answered her question. 'Most of the younger men aren't interested in farming nowadays so a lot of the farms around here are finding it difficult to hire workers. That's one of the reasons why Peter decided to get rid of his sheep. Apparently, goats are easier to deal with—not that you'd think so after today's little episode!'

He made a determined effort to appear upbeat as they collected the picnic hamper and drove back to Teedale but as he drew up outside the cottage, he couldn't help wishing there was some way he could reassure her that she didn't need to be so wary of him. He would never hurt her in any way, shape or form although he doubted if she would believe that so in the end he resorted to the good old standby of work because it was simpler.

'Hopefully, you'll have a better idea of the lie of the land after today.'

'It's been a big help,' she assured him politely before she turned to Daniel. 'Thank you for having me on your team. I really enjoyed my first ever game of football.'

'We could have another match tomorrow if you like,' Daniel said eagerly. 'You could come for lunch and we could play footie afterwards.'

'Oh…um…that's really kind of you but I have things to do tomorrow.'

'We'll fix something up another time,' Alex put in hastily because it was obvious that the thought of spending another day in their company was more than she could stomach.

His spirits, already low, plummeted even further at the thought and he realised that it was time he brought the outing to an end. 'I'll see you on Monday. Enjoy the rest of your weekend.'

'You, too.' She got out of the car then paused. 'Before I forget, shall I cover any calls that come in tonight?'

'That would be great. I'll switch the surgery phone through to the cottage so the calls will go directly to you.' He managed a fairly passable laugh. 'I can have a glass of wine tonight with my sausage and mash and not feel guilty!'

She smiled faintly. 'Really pushing the boat out, aren't you?'

'It's non-stop fun and excitement being a country GP.'

He gave her a quick wave then drove away, stopping briefly at the surgery where he diverted any incoming phone calls to the cottage. It was gone five by the time they'd unloaded the car so he sent Daniel upstairs to wash off some of the grime while he peeled the potatoes for their tea. Once Daniel had finished in the bathroom, it was his turn.

Alex showered and changed into clean clothes and was just going back downstairs when the doorbell chimed. He sighed as he veered off to answer it. Although he'd told Francesca that she could cover any calls that night, he could hardly refuse if someone turned up at his door...

He blinked when he opened the door and found Francesca standing on the step because she was the last person he'd expected to see.

'I'm really sorry to bother you, Alex, but I need your help.'

CHAPTER NINE

IT WAS the breakthrough he'd been praying for, Alex realised giddily.

'I know,' he said huskily because his heart was thumping like a jackhammer.

'You do?' She looked blankly at him. 'But I've only just seen the state of the place so how do you know about the leak?'

'Leak?'

'Yes. The whole ground floor of the cottage is flooded.' She swept her hand down her legs and his eyes widened when he realised that the bottoms of her jeans were soaking wet. 'That's why I need to know where to find the stopcock to turn off the water.'

'It's in the cupboard next to the chimney breast,' he explained, frantically trying to switch gears. 'I'll come and take a look at it. It's bound to be stiff and you mightn't be able to turn it off. Just give me a moment to fetch some tools...'

'There's no need. I can do it now that I know where to find it. I just need the phone number of a local plumber now so I can get him to fix the pipe.'

'We don't have a plumber in the village. The nearest one is in Ashbourne and I don't rate your chances very highly if you're hoping to get him out on a Saturday night,' he said firmly, pushing his feet into his wellies. 'It will probably be Monday before you can get anyone to come out here.'

'Oh. I didn't realise that.' She bit her lip and he sighed because her reluctance to accept his help was really starting

119

to get him down, especially after having his hopes raised like that.

'I'm only offering to turn off the water, Francesca. I'm not trying to force you into some sort of compromising position if that's what you're worried about.'

'Of course not! I just don't want to be a nuisance.'

'You aren't.'

He glanced round when Daniel came into the hall, glad of the distraction because he didn't want to say something he might regret. If he'd hoped their heart-to-heart the other night might have cleared the air, he'd have been sadly mistaken. If anything, she seemed more prickly than ever and it was frustrating to have to contend with her continued wariness.

'I'm just popping over to the cottage,' he told his son. 'A pipe has burst and Francesca has water all over her floor. Do you want to come with us or will you stay here? I should only be a few minutes.'

'I'd rather stay here.' Daniel grinned at him. 'And I won't open the door or mess with the stove so you don't have to tell me not to.'

'Good. I'll save my breath in case I need it for snorkelling around the cottage,' he replied, making swimming gestures with his arms, much to Daniel's amusement.

He closed the front door and fetched his toolbox from the garage then accompanied Francesca back to the cottage. The living-room floor was several inches deep in water and he groaned when he saw the mess it had made. 'Do you have any idea where it's coming from?'

'Under the kitchen sink. It's pouring out of one of the pipes.'

She took him into the kitchen and showed him the source of the leak. Alex crouched down, taking care not to brush against her as he examined the pipe. He sighed under his breath because he'd never gone to such lengths to avoid contact before and it simply proved how serious this situation was becoming. He'd lived like a monk since Trish had died and had never once been tempted by the thought of having a physical relationship with another woman, yet the slightest contact with Francesca made him ache with longing.

'It looks as though the whole pipe's corroded so it will need replacing.' He tapped the pipe with a spanner and frowned when he heard the dull thud of metal. 'It's the original lead piping, too, so that probably means the whole cottage is connected up with lead pipes.'

'Is that a problem?'

'In as much as it will all need changing, yes, it is.'

He stood up and went back to the living room, opening the cupboard beside the chimney breast to find the stopcock. The tap was stiff from lack of use but a couple of thumps with a wrench eventually paid off and he was able to turn off the water.

'Will it be a difficult job to upgrade the pipework?' Francesca asked anxiously.

'More inconvenient than anything else. The floors will need to come up so the plumber can get at the pipes.'

'Can't he just repair the pipe that's leaking? The rest seem to be all right so what's the point of changing them all?'

'Because of the risk of lead poisoning.' He shrugged. 'I should have had the plumbing checked before you moved in but I never thought about it.'

'It isn't your fault. It's just one of those things.' She looked around the living room and shook her head. 'It's going to make a terrible mess if the plumber has to pull up all these floorboards.'

'I'll make sure that everything is put back in its rightful place. And it goes without saying that I'll pay for the work to be done,' he added. 'It is my responsibility.'

'Even so, it was generous to include the cottage as part

of my package and I'd prefer to pay for this. Maybe we can come to some sort of arrangement—you can deduct a set amount from my salary each month to cover the cost of the work.'

'If that's what you want.' There was no point arguing when he knew why she was so determined to pay for the work to be done. She didn't want to be beholden to him and it simply proved how futile it was to hope that they could ever grow closer. She'd been too badly hurt to risk her heart being broken a second time and there was no point telling her that he wouldn't hurt her because she wouldn't believe him. They'd reached an impasse and, quite frankly, he didn't know where to go from here.

'That's about all we can do for now. Hopefully, the plumber will be able to come out on Monday and sort everything out. In the meantime, you'd better pack while I go and see what Daniel's up to.'

'Pack?'

Fran was in the process of emptying a bucket of dirty water down the outside drain when Alex stuck his head out of the back door. She put the bucket on the ground and stared at him. 'Pack what?'

'Clothes, make-up…whatever you need to tide you over the weekend. We can fetch the rest of your things later. Once they start ripping out the old pipes the whole place will be in a terrible mess….'

'Hang on a moment—I seem to be missing something. Why do I need clothes to tide me over the weekend?'

'Because you can't stay here. There's no water for cooking or washing—no toilet facilities even—so you'll have to stay with me until the plumbing is sorted out. Now I really must get back to Daniel.'

Fran opened her mouth to tell him that she had no intention of staying with him only she didn't get the chance because he'd already gone back inside. She hurried after him in time to see the front door closing as he left. There was no point going after him when he was anxious to get back to Daniel so she would tell him later that she wouldn't be accepting his hospitality. Maybe she didn't have any water but she'd manage…

Wouldn't she?

She groaned as she glanced down at her filthy clothes and did a reality check. How on earth was she going to carry on living in the cottage without any water? Maybe she didn't want to stay with Alex but what was the alternative? She could hardly turn up for surgery in this state!

She went upstairs and packed her overnight bag. It was just gone six when she left the cottage to walk the short distance to Alex's house. He'd left the door on the latch so she didn't bother knocking before she let herself in. He was in the kitchen and she steeled herself when he looked round, feeling her stomach tying itself in knots with tension.

'Tea will be another ten minutes yet so there's plenty of time if you want a shower. You can use the bedroom you had the last time you stayed here. There's clean towels in the airing cupboard so help yourself.'

It was said very casually and she felt her anxiety ease a little. 'Thank you.'

'You're welcome.'

He tossed her a smile then returned his attention to the stove. Fran backtracked along the hall, experiencing a strange sense of déjà vu as she climbed the stairs and opened the bedroom door. Everything looked much the same as it had done the first time she'd stayed there and it was comforting in a way because nothing untoward had happened then so there was no reason to imagine anything would happen now. Alex was just helping out a colleague in difficulty and that was all there was to it.

By the time she went back downstairs a short time later,

she was feeling a little foolish about the way she'd reacted. Alex was just serving up their meal and he grinned at her.

'Amazing what a bit of soap and water can do to restore your spirits.'

'It is.' She returned his smile then glanced away as her heart gave a treacherous little hiccup when she saw the warmth in his gaze. 'Can I do anything to help?'

'Not really… Oh, yes. Could you get the water? There's one of those filter jugs in the fridge and the glasses are in the cupboard above my head.'

'Sure.'

Fran went to the fridge and took out the jug of water. Alex was spooning mashed potato onto the plates so she edged around him to reach the cupboard…. Her breasts brushed against him and she sucked in her breath when she felt her nipples immediately harden. All she had on was a cotton T-shirt and she was achingly conscious of the way her nipples were protruding through the soft fabric.

She swiftly collected the glasses and took them to the table, keeping her back to him until she was sure her hormones had settled down, but she couldn't pretend that she wasn't worried about what had happened. She wanted to keep Alex on the very margins of her life but it was proving extremely difficult to do that and it scared her to know that she was attracted to him after what had happened with Paul. She couldn't afford to make another mistake but how could she be sure that what she was feeling was real and not just a reaction to what had gone on? She was too vulnerable at the moment to assess the situation properly so she had to be very careful and keep her distance from him no matter how difficult it might prove to be.

Alex was very conscious of the undercurrents as he sat down at the table and he had a good idea what was causing them, too. He'd felt Francesca's response when she'd accidentally brushed against him and was having his own problems dealing with what had happened. He'd never considered the fact that she might be attracted to him. She was always so cool towards him that it hadn't occurred to him that she might feel this way. Now it was the sweetest kind of torment to remember how her nipples had pushed so invitingly against him…

'Dad, you're not listening to me!'

'Sorry.' He hastily dragged his thoughts back to the real world when he heard the plaintive note in his son's voice. 'What did you say again?'

'I *said* that now Fran can have that other game of football with us,' Daniel repeated wearily.

'Yes, of course she can,' he agreed, feeling even more guilty for letting his mind wander. He paid Daniel far too little attention as it was without wasting his time speculating about whether or not Francesca was attracted to him. So maybe she *had* reacted to that moment of intimacy but he knew enough about the human body to understand that it hadn't necessarily meant anything. His spirits plummeted and he had to dredge up a smile for Daniel's benefit.

'We can have a rematch tomorrow, if you like.'

'Brill!'

Daniel immediately cheered up at the prospect of the coming match and chattered on about who would be on which team. Alex joined in the discussion although he was aware that Francesca had very little to say on the subject.

He shot her a wary glance and felt heat run through him when he discovered that she was watching him. There was a moment when their eyes met before she lowered her gaze but he'd seen enough to know that she was as on edge as he was. Quite frankly, he wasn't sure if it made him feel better or worse to know that. He didn't enjoy having her blank him but how did he handle her new-found awareness of him? Should he try to use it to his advantage and possibly run the risk of alienating her even more, or should he play safe and pretend nothing had happened?

He groaned because there were no easy answers to this dilemma. He would just have to rely on his instincts and hope they wouldn't let him down!

'Prump!' Alex sat back in his seat with a triumphant smile. 'Add that to my score and I rather think that makes me the winner.'

'Prump? *Prump!* There's no such word!'

Fran pushed aside her pile of letter tiles in disgust. It was ten o'clock and they were in the final throes of a hard-fought game of Scrabble. Alex had suggested they should play after Daniel had gone to bed and she'd been only too happy to agree because it had been a safe way to pass the evening. However, safe or not, there was no way that she was letting him get away with cheating.

'Show me the entry in the dictionary which states that ''prump'' is a real word.'

'Don't you trust me?' he demanded, looking hurt.

'No, I don't! You've come up with some really dodgy words tonight and I've let you have them, but you're not getting away with this.' She folded her arms and stared at him. 'If ''prump'' is a real word, what does it mean?'

'It's Old English so that's probably why you haven't heard it before. It's a contraction of the words ''primp'' and ''plump''.'

'Really?' She frowned as she digested that bit of information then gasped when he chuckled. 'You made that up, didn't you? There's no such word as ''prump''—just as I thought!'

'No, but I managed to convince *you* there was, didn't I?'

'You *nearly* did,' she amended haughtily. 'I had my doubts all along.'

'Oh, come on, admit it. If I hadn't given the game away,

you'd have believed me. You're just too gullible, Fran. That's your trouble.'

The accusation stung far more than he'd intended it to. Fran tried to hide her dismay as she scooped the letter tiles into the box but he'd obviously realised what he'd said.

'Sorry,' he said softly, leaning forward so that she was forced to look at him. 'I didn't mean to hit a raw nerve.'

'You didn't.' She put the lid on the box and stood up. 'Anyway, I've had enough excitement for one night so I think I'll go to bed.'

She hurried to the door, trying not to think about what he'd said but it was impossible not to. She *was* gullible— extremely so if past events were anything to go by—and it hurt to be reminded what a fool she'd been.

'Stop it.'

She looked round when Alex spoke. 'I beg your pardon?'

'Stop blaming yourself because you were taken in by what Paul Bryant told you.' He got up and came towards her and she could see the compassion in his eyes. 'You had no reason to believe he wasn't telling you the truth, did you?'

'No, but—'

'But nothing.' He took hold of her by the shoulders and gave her a gentle shake. 'A lot of people fell for his trickery, not just you, so he must have been extremely convincing.'

'He was,' she said slowly because she'd never considered that fact before. She certainly wasn't the only one who'd believed in Paul. Hundreds of people had believed his lies so why was she any more at fault than them. They were *all* victims of a highly successful con man.

'Then stop torturing yourself. It wasn't your fault, Fran…none of it!'

He gave her another little shake then let her go, as though he was afraid that he might have overstepped the mark. Fran summoned a smile but she couldn't believe how simple it all was. With just a few words, Alex had managed to make her feel better about herself than she'd done in ages.

'Thank you,' she said quietly but sincerely.

'All part of the service.'

He grinned at her but there was something about the expression in his eyes that made her heart start to race. She turned away, terrified of doing the wrong thing. Maybe Alex had helped her to see that she wasn't to blame for what had happened but she mustn't let herself get carried away. She was still very vulnerable and couldn't afford to rush headlong into another situation she might not be able to handle.

'I think I'll have an early night as well.' He switched off the lights and followed her into the hall. 'It's been a busy day....' He broke off when the telephone suddenly rang and groaned. 'And it isn't over yet by the sound of it.'

Fran waited by the stairs as he went to answer the phone because if it was a call from a patient, it would be her job to respond. She listened while he had a brief conversation with the caller and could tell from his tone that it wasn't good news. She was already prepared for the worst when he hung up.

'That was the cave search and rescue team controller. There's a party of injured cavers trapped below ground. One of the group managed to find his way out and raised the alarm, but the rescue team don't want to risk moving the others until they know if it's safe to do so. I'm going over there to see what I can do.'

'At this time of the night,' she exclaimed.

'It makes little difference what time of day it is when you're below ground. From what I can gather, one of the men is in a pretty bad way. He fell about thirty feet down an underground chute and injured his back. The other two aren't so badly hurt, but they'll need checking over before they're moved.'

'Has the rescue team requested an ambulance?' she put in as he unhooked his coat from the peg.

'Yes, but it will be almost an hour before the paramedics get there. The air ambulance crew is on standby, too, so they'll be able to ferry the guy with the back injury straight to hospital. It's no joke, transporting someone with a spinal injury over this kind of terrain,' he added grimly.

'Shall I come with you?' she offered impulsively, wondering if she was mad to suggest it. She knew that he didn't expect her to go along but she also knew that he'd be under a lot of pressure if he had to deal with several casualties by himself.

'It would be a big help, of course, but are you sure you want to come? If you've not been caving before, your first time underground can be a bit daunting.'

'I'll be fine,' she assured him, trying not to think about what lay in store. 'What about Daniel, though? We can't leave him in the house on his own.'

'Mrs Blake from next door will come over and stay with him. It's what normally happens when I get called out at night. I'll just phone her.'

He picked up the receiver while Fran ran upstairs to get ready. She knew it would be cold outside so she pulled a sweater over her T-shirt then added a fleece jacket and an extra pair of socks. Alex was standing by the front door when she went back downstairs, waiting for his neighbour to arrive. The elderly lady appeared a few minutes later, brushing aside his thanks and assuring him that she was happy to stay as long as he needed her. He got her settled then checked they had everything they needed.

'You'd better put this on.' He handed Fran the waxed jacket she'd used once before. 'It will be bitterly cold out on the hills at this time of the year so you'll need a hat and gloves as well.'

He gave her a woolly hat and some gloves and she put

them on without a murmur. He was the expert and she certainly wasn't going to question his orders.

There was a strong easterly wind blowing when they went out to the car and she gratefully scurried into the passenger seat. They left the village and drove towards Ashbourne, turning onto a narrow track that wound its way through the lower reaches of the hills.

'The entrance to the caves is just around the next bend but we're going straight to Solomon's Chute because that's where the cavers ended up,' he explained, changing gear as they lurched over the rough terrain.

Fran clutched hold of the doorhandle to steady herself. 'Can we get into the caves from there?'

'Yes, but it's a very difficult descent and certainly too difficult for you to attempt it.'

Another gear change, another lurch, and this time she lost her grip and went cannoning into him. He quickly steadied her, his hand resting on her arm for only as long as it took her to recover her balance, but even that was enough to start her heart racing. Fran scooted back to her side of the car, clamping her fingers around the handle to avoid any further mishaps.

'As I was saying, it's far too difficult for you to enter the caves via the chute.'

His voice hummed with tension and she bit her lip because there was no point pretending that she didn't know what had caused it. He was as aware of her as she was of him and it was scary to realise it—far more terrifying than the prospect of entering the underground caverns. It took her all her time to reply with a semblance of normality but even then she could hear the strain in her voice.

'So how am I going to get in?'

'There's another entrance close by. I'll get one of the guys to take you in that way. It will be much easier for you.'

He swung the car round a final bend and lurched to a stop. Fran gasped when she saw that the whole hillside ahead of them was lit up by floodlights. There were a lot of people milling about—members of the rescue team, she assumed—as well as a number of vehicles. It was a full-scale alert and her stomach churned with nerves as Alex parked the car and turned to her.

'Just do exactly what you're told and you'll be fine, Fran. I don't want you to take any risks, though. Promise me?'

'Promise,' she repeated huskily because it was impossible to pretend that she hadn't heard the concern in his voice.

'Good.'

He leant over and kissed her lightly on the cheek then swung himself out of the car. Fran put her hand to her face, feeling the warmth of his lips through the thickness of her glove. It was the sort of kiss a friend might have bestowed on her and yet the ramifications of it went way beyond friendship. Alex had kissed her despite her attempts to keep him at a distance. He'd kissed her knowing that she wouldn't welcome his attentions. He'd ignored all the reasons why he shouldn't have kissed her because his motive for doing so had overridden everything else.

He'd kissed her because he *cared* about her and all of a sudden it felt as though the layer of ice that had enclosed her heart since Paul's defection had started to melt.

'Bob is going to guide you to the bottom of the chute to meet me. Just do exactly what he tells you to do and you'll be fine.'

'What about you?'

Fran tried to keep the worry out of her voice but it was hard not to let panic creep in. They were standing at the top of Solomon's Chute which had turned out to be a narrow fissure in the ground barely wide enough for a man to squeeze through. A series of ropes and pulleys had been set up over the mouth of the vertical tunnel and she watched in dismay as Alex attached his harness to one of the lines.

'I'm going down there to see how badly injured they are,' he explained calmly, fastening the metal clips that would anchor him to the ropes. 'Hopefully, I'll have a better idea of the situation by the time you arrive.'

'Is one of the team going with you?' she asked, peering into the black pit and quickly looking away as a wave of nausea hit her. She'd never thought about going underground before and had no idea if she was claustrophobic. However, she had to admit that she was growing increasingly uneasy about how she would cope with the experience.

'There's not enough room. With three men already down there, there'll be barely enough room for me as it is. With a bit of luck, we'll be able to move the least severely injured out of the way to give us some room to manoeuvre.'

He broke off when one of the rescue team came over to him. Fran frowned when she heard him swear softly because it was obvious that something else had happened. His face was set when he turned to her again.

'We're going to have to get a move on. Apparently, there's rain forecast tonight so we need to get the casualties out as quickly as possible.'

'Why?' She clutched hold of his arm when he started to lower himself into the hole. 'What difference will it make if it rains, Alex?'

'The cavern at the bottom of the chute could flood.'

He nodded to the winchman then slithered into the hole. Fran pressed her hand to her mouth as she watched him disappear from sight. She knew it was silly but she couldn't help feeling tearful.

'The doc knows what he's doing,' Bob told her kindly, patting her arm. 'He'll be fine, love, you'll see.'

She managed a wobbly smile, feeling a bit embarrassed about revealing her feelings. She followed Bob away from the chute and, on his instructions, shed her jacket and slipped on a pair of orange overalls. A helmet with a miner's lamp attached to the front came next then a leather belt that held some of the same metal clips which Alex had used to secure himself to the rope. Bob checked their equipment then led her down the path to where another floodlight had been set up. Fran could see quite a large cave cut into the hillside and gulped. Despite the bright lights, the place looked very dark and uninviting.

'You'll be fine,' Bob assured her. 'It's an easy enough route from here so you shouldn't have any problems.'

Fran could only hope he wasn't being overly optimistic. However, she knew it wasn't the time to voice her doubts. She switched on the light on her helmet and followed him into the cavern. It was much bigger than she'd expected it to be and there were a number of passageways leading from it. Bob chose the middle tunnel on their right, ducking down to avoid banging his head on the roof as they entered the narrow passage.

'It's not too bad at first,' he shouted back to her. 'It's only the last stretch that you'll need to crawl.'

She murmured something in reply, not wanting him to know how scared she was. The earth seemed to be pressing in on her from all sides and it was a horrible feeling, especially as the light on her helmet was only strong enough to illuminate a small area directly in front of her. They made their way along the tunnel for what seemed like miles to her before Bob slowed as they came to a bend.

'This is where we're going to have to crawl. Keep your head down, Doc, because there's not much of a gap between you and the roof. I wouldn't want you to brain yourself.'

His cheery tone belied their situation. Fran guessed it was just routine to him but she'd never experienced anything like it before. Sweat broke out all over her body as she dropped onto her hands and knees and crawled along the tunnel.

When she tried to lift her head, her helmet rapped against the roof, unleashing a shower of grit onto her. She'd just reached a point when she was sure she couldn't go any further when the tunnel suddenly widened and lights appeared up ahead. A few seconds later, they were at the bottom of the chute and Alex was there, smiling at her.

'Dr Livingstone, I presume?'

'Sadly not, although I can understand why the good doctor decided to take his chances in the jungle,' she replied tartly, struggling to her feet. 'I'd give anything for a glimpse of a tree right now!'

Alex laughed, his hazel eyes filled with such warmth that the horrors of the journey suddenly faded into insignificance as she basked in its glow. 'You're doing great, Fran. I know how scary it must have been for you because it's your first time underground. I'm really proud of you.'

Fran felt a bubble of happiness float to the surface of her mind at his praise. Maybe she *was* stuck at the bottom of a hole in the ground but Alex was with her and that made a world of difference.

'Thank you.'

'You're welcome.'

One last super-warm smile before he turned his attention to the casualties but it was more than enough to help her through what might lie ahead. They worked in harmony after that—Alex carried on attending to the caver who'd suffered the spinal injury while she concentrated on the other two men. One had a broken ankle but was otherwise unhurt so she strapped up his ankle and he was winched up the chute.

The other man had suffered a head injury and was showing definite signs of concussion: he was drowsy and unresponsive, and his eyes dilated unevenly when she shone a light into them. She'd just finished examining him when he suffered a convulsion so she quickly rolled him onto his side and placed him in the recovery position.

She checked him again once it was over and it was obvious that his level of consciousness had deteriorated dramatically. There could be swelling inside his skull caused by a build-up of fluid or blood and he needed urgent treatment if he was to have a chance of surviving.

'He needs to be transferred to hospital immediately,' she told Alex. 'Can I get the helicopter to take him while you're dealing with your patient?'

'Yes, that's fine. I still need to stabilise this guy before we can risk moving him so you carry on.'

Fran turned to Bob, who'd been waiting inside the tunnel to give them room to work. 'Can you call for the helicopter? We need to get this man to hospital. Tell them it's a serious head trauma which will require surgery.'

'Will do, Doc.'

She left him to make the arrangements, her anxiety increasing when the casualty suffered a second seizure. She administered a sedative and got him ready to be moved—fitting him with a neck brace and padding the wound on his head with extra layers of gauze. She wasn't happy about his being hauled up the chute but it would take too long to get him out of the cave by any other route so as soon as she was sure that she'd done everything possible for him, she helped Bob to rig up the harness.

Getting the casualty up to the surface was incredibly difficult because he was unconscious and unable to help himself. Bob followed him up, helping to ease him around any obstacles, but her heart was in her mouth as she watched the ascent. It was a relief when they reached the top but even then the job wasn't over. There was still the caver with the spinal injury to attend to so she went over to Alex and crouched beside him.

'How's he doing?'

'Not too good. There's definite signs of misalignment in both the thoracic and lumbar spines,' he told her grimly. 'I've given him methylprednisolone because it's known to improve recovery from spinal cord damage, but it's not a miracle cure. The cord may be too badly damaged for all I know. Feel for yourself and you'll see what I mean.'

She carefully slid her hand beneath the man's back and grimaced when she felt the vertebrae bulging out of place. 'It's going to be really risky moving him in this state.'

'We don't have a choice.' He finished administering an injection of analgesic before he looked at her. 'One of the guys just radioed down to say that it's started raining. I was hoping it would hold off a bit longer but we're out of luck.'

'Will this section of the caverns flood?' she asked anxiously, looking round.

'Yes. The area around Solomon's Chute is one of the worst for flooding. There's an underground stream which runs through this whole network of caves. The water table is always high at this time of the year so it won't need much of a downpour to start it seeping into here. Let's hope we can get him shifted before that happens.'

'And if we can't?'

'Then we'll have to come up with another solution.'

Fran couldn't think of anything to say to that. The thought of them being trapped underground by rising flood water was more than enough to contend with. She helped him finish stabilising the caver and then Bob came back with a couple of other members of the rescue team. Between them they managed to move the man into a special spinal cradle, strapping him firmly into place to minimise the risk of causing any further damage to his spine during the transfer. As soon as they'd finished, Bob told them they would have to move to a cave further along the network of caverns. Although it would take them longer to get the casualty out via that route, it would mean they could avoid being trapped by flood water.

Fran followed the convoy along the passage. It was only slightly higher than the one she'd come along before and it wasn't easy to manoeuvre the stretcher through it. They reached the cave at last and stopped while she and Alex checked their patient again. Alex decided to give him another shot of analgesic and he'd just finished when one of the group shouted to warn them there was water seeping into the tunnel they'd just travelled along. Bob immediately got on the radio and arranged for some more men to come and help them get the casualty to safety.

'It'll be all right.' Alex sat back on his heels and looked at her. 'Even if the water gets into here, it won't rise very much. There's a run-off at the far side so it would need a spell of really bad weather before this section flooded.'

'Good. I can't say that I relish the idea of underground swimming lessons,' she replied, trying to make a joke of their predicament.

'It would be another first for you,' he teased. 'Something else you could write in your diary and look back on in years to come.'

'Pass! I'm perfectly happy leading a normal, boring life, thank you very much.'

'I don't think you could ever be boring, Fran.'

There was something in his voice which made her nerves hum. She didn't say anything as she bent over the patient because she wasn't sure how to deal with what was happening. She didn't want to be so aware of Alex but she couldn't stop responding to him: a smile, a touch, a gentle kiss and all her good intentions floated away and it scared her to admit how she felt. Even though she knew that he wasn't like Paul, there were no guarantees that she wouldn't get hurt again.

CHAPTER TEN

THE next hour was a taxing time for everyone and Alex was glad when it was over. Getting the stretcher along the narrow tunnels was a test of endurance for them all. He was on edge as he constantly reminded everyone how vital it was not to jar the injured caver. With an unstable spinal injury, such as this, the slightest movement could result in paralysis, so he harped on and on about the need for caution until he was as sick of hearing himself as everyone else must have been.

It was almost one o'clock when they finally surfaced to a round of applause from the other members of the team. The helicopter was waiting to transfer the casualty to the nearest spinal injury unit so they wasted no time loading him on board. The caver, a young man called Liam Harris, was conscious by then and he gripped Alex's hand.

'Thanks, Doc. No matter what happens from here on, I'm truly grateful for everything you've done.'

'Glad to be of help,' Alex said, mentally crossing his fingers as to what the outcome would be.

'Fingers crossed the surgeons will be able to do something for him.'

He glanced round when Francesca came to join him, inwardly sighing when he realised the same thought had been going through her mind as well as his. He would love to take it as a sign of their increasing harmony but he was afraid to read too much into it. She may have been less prickly tonight but probably circumstances had dictated the change in her attitude. It would be silly to get his hopes up that it marked an upturn in their relationship.

'Amen,' he endorsed with deliberate lightness as the helicopter lifted off. The rest of the team were getting ready to go home so he had a word with Bob then said his farewells. There would need to be an inquest at some point but it was too late to worry about that now. Francesca yawned widely as they climbed into the car and he chuckled.

'Keeping you up, are we?'

'You certainly are. I'm usually tucked up in bed by this hour of the night—or, rather, morning.'

Alex didn't say anything because he didn't want her to know how the comment had affected him. Thinking about how she would look in bed was something he mustn't dwell on. However, it was impossible not to think about it, especially when she fell asleep on the way home and ended up with her head resting on his shoulder.

He groaned as he imagined how wonderful it would be to take her to his bed. She would hold back at first because she wouldn't want to give too much of herself away but he sensed that beneath the cool façade there was a wealth of passion lying dormant. If he could convince her to put aside her fears and trust him their love-making would be unlike anything they'd experienced before. It would be the meeting of equals, both of them giving and taking their pleasure. The thought almost tipped him over the edge so that it was difficult to respond calmly when he drew up in front of the house and she woke up.

'Oh!' She quickly straightened, a touch of colour running up her cheeks. 'You should have woken me up.'

'And spoil your beauty sleep?' He summoned a smile because there was no way he could let her know what had been occupying his thoughts. 'I'm not that brave!'

He opened the car door, suddenly eager to bring the night to an end. He should have himself in hand by morning, be less likely to do anything foolish. After all, he didn't want to make his life any more difficult by letting her know that he was attracted to her...

He frowned because for some reason that sentiment didn't quite ring true. Although he didn't deny that he was attracted to her, was it only physical desire he felt? He searched his heart as they made their way up the path but it was surprisingly difficult to answer the question. Whilst there was no doubt in his mind that Francesca was a stunningly beautiful woman and that any man would want to be with her, he sensed there was more to it than that.

Was it possible that he was falling in love with her?

Alex's stomach lurched because he'd never considered the fact that he might fall in love again. He simply hadn't believed it was possible to find love more than once in a lifetime yet he could no longer rule out it happening. It made him see that he had to take a long hard look at his feelings because it wasn't just his life that would be affected if it was true but Daniel's as well.

It had taken Daniel a long time to come to terms with Trish's death. He only had to remember the nights when he'd held his son in his arms and rocked him to sleep after yet another nightmare had woken him to know how hard it had been for Daniel to get over what had happened. He couldn't begin to imagine how Daniel would react if he tried to introduce another woman into their life. He might be perfectly happy with the idea or he might reject it completely and Alex simply wasn't prepared to take that risk at the moment. He had to be very sure of what he was doing before he disrupted Daniel's life, confident of what the outcome would be—and that was the one thing he couldn't claim to be.

He sighed as he unlocked the back door because even if his feelings for Francesca were deeper than he'd imagined them to be, it might be safer to keep them to himself.

*   *   *

'I've just spoken to the consultant at the spinal unit. Liam Harris has regained some feeling in the lower part of his body.'

Fran looked up when Alex poked his head round the door to her consulting room. It was Wednesday morning and she was just about to make a start on her list. There'd been a queue of people in the waiting room when she'd arrived so it looked like it was going to be another busy day which suited her fine. She wanted to fill up her time with work so there was no room for anything else.

'That's good news,' she said, smiling at him.

'Isn't it just.'

He returned her smile although she couldn't help noticing the lack of animation in his expression. It wasn't the first time she'd been aware of it either, because ever since they'd returned from rescuing those cavers, he'd seemed very subdued. She had wondered if it had been a conscious decision to keep things low-key while she was staying at his house but he'd been just as distant during working hours and it bothered her. Why *was* Alex deliberately trying to keep her at arm's length?

'Anyway, the consultant has promised to keep us posted so let's hope Liam will continue to make progress.'

'Yes,' she agreed, following his lead and keeping her tone as neutral as his had been.

'We've also had the lab results back for Peter Arkwright. I asked them to fax them to us and they've just arrived. Take a look at this.'

He handed her a sheet of paper and waited while she read it. Fran gasped in amazement at what she was seeing.

'Brucellosis! But I thought it had been eradicated from British livestock years ago.'

'It had, so I wonder how Peter has managed to contract it?' Alex frowned as he took the sheet from her again and studied it. 'There's no doubt about the findings because the blood sample showed a strain of the *Brucella* bacterium. I've asked the lab to see if they can trace its origins. They'll know if there's been any other outbreaks in the country because it's a notifiable disease,' he explained. 'So they might be able to match it.'

'It's often present in goats, isn't it?' Fran said slowly. 'I remember reading about an incident in Greece last year. Apparently, cheese made from unpasturised goats' milk was to blame.'

'So you think Peter might have caught it from one of his animals? I wonder if he's added to his herd recently, maybe imported livestock from another EU country?'

'It's possible. Why don't you ask him?'

'Oh, I shall. This needs sorting out as quickly as possible. I'll need to take Peter some antibiotics so I'll call at the farm on my way to Ashbourne. Did I mention that there's yet another meeting about next year's budget this afternoon?'

'No, but it isn't a problem. There's not that many people booked in for smear tests this afternoon so I'll be able to get them done after I've finished the house calls.'

'Thanks.' He grimaced. 'I feel as though I'm dumping a lot of extra work onto you.'

'That's what I'm here for,' she said lightly. 'To make your life that bit easier.'

'Mmm.'

He didn't say anything else but she saw the way his mouth had tightened and knew that her comment had hit a nerve. She sighed as he went away because she hated to think that she might not be making life any easier for him. Alex had been working far too hard in the past few years and she wanted to relieve some of the pressure off him.

And that was all? a small voice whispered slyly. She wanted to lighten his workload and nothing else?

She shook her head to rid herself of the disquieting idea

that she would like to do a lot more for him than simply improve his working week. There was a time and a place for thoughts like that and this wasn't one of them!

The morning flew past with the usual assortment of complaints—colds, headaches, a positive pregnancy test that was greeted with delight by the patient when she gave her the news. Mary had a list of home visits for her to do once surgery ended so Fran took herself off, wasting no time because there were the afternoon appointments to get through when she came back.

She was a little late arriving back at the surgery because her last patient, old Tom Carter's wife, had insisted she have a cup of tea with them. Fortunately, Hilary Johnson, their practice nurse, had everything ready for her when Fran raced into the consulting room.

'Sorry I'm late. I got held up at the Carters' house. Mrs Carter insisted I have a cup of tea with them.'

'My, you are honoured. Not many people get invited in for a cuppa so what's your secret?' Hilary asked, smiling at her. An attractive widow in her fifties with softly greying brown hair, she'd proved to be a great help since Fran had joined the practice. Now Fran laughed.

'I'm not sure but I think it could be the fact that Tom says I look just like his wife did when they were courting.'

Hilary laughed at that. 'It's hard to imagine so I'll have to take his word for it. They say love is blind, don't they?'

'I think it's sweet. They're obviously still devoted to one another after fifty years of marriage and you don't find that very often nowadays.'

'You certainly don't,' Hilary agreed, passing her a printed sheet of the names of the women who needed smear tests that day. 'Some folk seem to come up trumps and find their ideal mate and other people end up with the short end of the wedge.'

Like she'd done, Fran thought ruefully, although she didn't say so. Thankfully there was no time to dwell on it when there were patients waiting to be seen so she asked Hilary to call in their first appointment and set to work. Most of the women were delighted that she was doing their tests because they found it less embarrassing to have the procedure performed by another woman.

Fran took the samples, explained to each woman in turn that she would receive a letter from the screening centre informing her of the results, and then cleared up. She was just sealing the envelope of samples to take it to the post office when Mary tapped on the door.

'Sorry, Fran, but Bob Patterson from the cave rescue team is on the phone. Can you have a word with him?'

'Of course. I'll come to the office and take the call there,' she said immediately.

'I'll take this little lot to the post office,' Hilary offered.

'Oh, right, thanks.' She hurriedly made her way to the office and picked up the receiver. 'What can I do for you, Bob?'

'We've a bit of a problem, Doc. A teenager's gone missing and we think she may be in the caves close to Solomon's Chute. Apparently, there was a geology field trip to the area this morning for the kids from the high school. Nobody realised Sarah Robinson was missing until everyone was back on the coach and one of the other girls mentioned seeing her going into the tunnels.'

Fran's heart sank when she recognised the girl's name because Sarah was the girl she'd spoken to Alex about, the one who had been self-mutilating. Although she'd contacted Sarah's mother to set up an appointment for her daughter, Sarah hadn't visited the surgery yet. It would be unethical to explain that to Bob, however, so she concentrated on the main issue instead.

'So what are you planning on doing?'

'We're sending a team in to find her but it's not going to be easy because we're only guessing where she could be. The problem is that the caves are neck-deep in water in places and the kid is going to be very cold and wet when we find her.'

'Which is why you need my help.'

'Well, I was hoping to get Alex out here but Mary already explained that he's in Ashbourne. Would you mind very much coming along just in case we need a hand?'

'Of course not. Just tell me where to meet you and I'll make my way straight there.'

'If you can find your way to that big cavern where we entered the system the other night, that would save time,' Bob told her. 'Don't worry about clothes because I'll have a diving suit ready for you—not that you'll probably need it, mind,' he said quickly. 'It's just the best thing to wear to keep out the cold.'

'Right. Fine,' she said faintly, hoping he was telling her the truth.

She hung up and explained what was happening to Mary, shaking her head when the receptionist asked her if she should get a message to Alex to let him know where she was going.

'No, there's no need to worry him. It probably won't take that long and I'll be back before evening surgery. If you can just tell him that I'll be as quick as I can that will be fine.'

She left the surgery and hurried back to the cottage to change out of her skirt and blouse into a track suit which would be easier to replace when she got to the cavern. It only took her a few minutes and she set off again, switching on the windscreen wipers when it started raining as she left the village. It was very different, finding the route during the day, and she had to slow down in case she missed the turning but she recognised it immediately. Her car wasn't as suited to the rough terrain as Alex's had been and she groaned when she heard her exhaust rattling when it hit a bump. Another expensive repair was just what she needed!

Bob came hurrying over when she drew up and opened the car door for her. 'Thanks for coming, Doc. The good news is that we've found Sarah.'

'And the bad news?' Fran prompted, pulling up her coat collar as she got out of the car because it was pouring down now.

'The bad news is that she's refused to come out.'

Bob sighed as he guided her up the hillside. Fran nodded to some other members of the team she remembered from Saturday night then followed him into the main cavern.

'Do you know why she won't come out?' she asked.

'No. She's very upset—hysterical actually—so we were afraid to do anything which might make her move further into the caves. The further in you go, the deeper the water is,' he explained worriedly.

'Sarah has had a few problems recently,' she said carefully, not wanting to abuse her position of trust but needing to assure the girl's safety. 'Her mental state is very fragile.'

'Thank heavens we held off and didn't try to rush things,' Bob declared. 'So what do you suggest we do, Doc? We need to get her out as soon as possible if it's going to start raining hard.'

'I'll go and have a word with her, see if I can persuade her to come out,' Fran said, making up her mind. 'It would be best if there weren't too many people about so could you take me to her and let me deal with her?'

'Yes,' Bob said slowly and she could tell how reluctant he was.

'It might be the only way to get her out,' she explained because it was imperative that Sarah wasn't scared into doing anything silly.

'In that case we'll give it a go.'

Bob didn't argue as he went and took a black rubber diving suit out of a pile in the corner of the cavern. Fran kicked off her trainers and slipped out of the track suit so she could put it on. It was tight and uncomfortable but she didn't complain because Bob wouldn't have asked her to wear it if he hadn't thought it was necessary.

She put her shoes back on then fastened the strap on the helmet Bob gave her and turned on the light. They were entering the network of caverns via the same tunnel they'd used the previous Saturday but Fran could detect a change in the atmosphere as soon as they entered the passageway. The air smelled very dank and the ground underfoot was slippery with mud.

'Watch your step along here, Doc. The ground's not too good with all the rain we've had lately.'

Fran heeded the advice, moving carefully as she followed him. They came to the part where they had to crouch down and she steeled herself because inching along the muddy ground on her hands and knees wasn't a pleasant experience. They reached Solomon's Chute and stopped while Bob explained what was happening to his team-mates.

He turned to her. 'The girl's along that tunnel on the left. Apparently, she's sitting on a ledge and there's water beneath her—deep water, too, so be really careful what you're doing, Doc.'

'Will do.'

Fran managed to smile but her heart was in her mouth as she entered the tunnel. The light on her helmet rippled across the dank wet walls so that it felt as though she was wading through water. It was a relief when the tunnel widened and she saw Sarah up ahead. One of the team had set up a light so she turned off the light on her helmet before she moved any closer, stopping when the girl scrambled to her feet.

'There's no need to be scared, Sarah. I'm not going to

hurt you. I'm Francesca Goodwin and I'm a doctor at the surgery in Teedale. I know your mum, in fact.'

'Do you?' The teenager looked uncertainly at her, poised to flee if Fran did anything to alarm her, so she stayed quite still.

'Yes. She came to see me a couple of weeks ago because she's been having hot flushes. She said she's been driving you all mad by complaining about the heat.'

'And we're all freezing!' The girl suddenly smiled, her face looking pale and strained in the lamplight. 'Mum keeps turning off the central heating and dad keeps turning it back on!'

'What we women have to put up with!' Fran declared ruefully. 'You never think you'll be *that* age but it happens to all of us at some point, and me rather sooner than you!'

Sarah smiled shyly. 'You don't look that old. You don't look old enough to be a doctor, in fact.'

'Oh, thank you! Can I have that in writing, please, because I have to say that after the year I've had, I feel like an old crone!'

'Why? What happened?' Sarah said curiously, sitting back down on the ledge. Fran saw her shiver and knew it was imperative they got her out before hypothermia set in. All Sarah had on was a sweatshirt with a pair of jeans and it was freezing in the cavern.

'I fell in love with the wrong guy, would you believe?' She edged a little closer and was relieved when Sarah didn't jump up again.

'Why was he the wrong guy?'

'Because he didn't really love me. It's not just people your age who have problems, you see, Sarah. A lot of adults have them as well.'

'I s'ppose… But you can do something about your problems when you're grown-up, can't you?'

'You can try but you still need help to sort things out.

When you get really upset, it's difficult to think clearly, isn't it? Sometimes it helps to tell someone about your worries and let them give you advice.'

'Is that what happened to you?'

'Yes. I told Dr Shepherd about my problems and he helped me understand that what had happened wasn't my fault,' she replied truthfully, trying not to let her emotions surface when it struck her just how much Alex had helped her put everything into perspective.

'I don't know if anyone could help me,' Sarah said forlornly. 'I don't have any friends so I don't know who I can talk to.'

'You can tell me. I'm a good listener,' Fran said gently.

'You'll think I'm mad,' the girl muttered, burying her face in her arms.

'No. I think you're upset and need help. And that's something very different.'

'I...I keep cutting myself.' The girl bit her lip as she pushed up her sleeves and showed Fran the damage she'd done to her arms.

'Why do you do it, Sarah?'

'Because when I get really upset...really worried that I can't make things go right...it helps if I hurt myself.' She knuckled the tears from her eyes and sniffed. 'See. I told you I was crazy, didn't I? That's what the kids in school call me, Crazy Sarah!'

'You aren't crazy. There are hundreds of people like you who do the same thing. They believe it's the only way they can control what is happening to them, but there are other ways, I promise you. There are people who can help you, Sarah. You just need to ask and I'll arrange for you to see someone.'

'A psychiatrist, you mean? Then everyone will really know I'm mad, won't they?'

'No, because nobody will know apart from you and your

family. You aren't mad. You need help. If you had a tooth-ache you'd see a dentist and this is just the same.'

'You really believe that? It isn't just some rubbish to make me do what you want me to?' Sarah demanded.

'No. Cross my heart. Now, how about you come with me so we can go home and have a nice cup of hot chocolate to warm us up? I don't know about you, but I'm freezing!'

'OK.'

Sarah giggled as she stood up. Fran was just holding out her hand to help her off the ledge when there was a horrible cracking sound and the next minute Sarah was plunging into the water below them as the rock gave way. Fran screamed as the girl's head disappeared beneath the surface. Without stopping to think about the danger she might be putting herself in, she leapt into the pool after her, gasping when icy water splashed into her face. She couldn't see any sign of Sarah at first then all of a sudden she spotted her head bobbing above the water and swam over to her.

'Doc! Doc! Where are you!'

Bob came rushing into the cave but she couldn't answer him because she needed all her strength to keep herself and Sarah afloat. There seemed to be some kind of current pull-ing them into the middle of the pool and she knew that she had to stay near the edge. She managed to grab hold of an outcrop of rock and hung on, hoping that Bob wouldn't take too long to get them out because even with the diving suit, the water was bitterly cold.

She could just imagine the dressing-down she'd get from Alex when he heard what had happened. She was proving more a liability than a help and she wouldn't be surprised if he didn't send her packing—only she hoped he wouldn't because she didn't want to leave. All of a sudden what she wanted seemed so wonderfully clear. She wanted to stay in Teedale and make her home here.

With Alex.

For ever.

CHAPTER ELEVEN

ALEX was on his way back from the meeting when he heard the news about what had happened on the radio. Pulling over to the side of the road, he listened in horror as the announcer explained that there was a second rescue attempt being carried out at Solomon's Chute and that one of the local doctors who'd been involved in Saturday's incident was helping again that day.

He swung the car around, uncaring that he'd be late for afternoon surgery because this was far more important. It took him ten minutes to reach the turn-off for the caves and his heart was banging away so hard by that point that it was a wonder it didn't leap right out of his chest. So much for handling the situation coolly and calmly, he thought grimly. Fran might be in danger and a team of wild horses wouldn't keep him from her!

He ground the car to a stop and raced hell for leather up the hill to the main cavern where the search and rescue team had set up their base.

'What's happening?' he demanded. 'Where's Fran?'

'She's inside,' one of the men told him.

'Then I'm going in to see what I can do,' he said immediately.

'I don't know if you should,' the man cautioned. 'Doc Goodwin told Bob that she thought it best if she dealt with the girl by herself...'

'You don't mean to say that she's in there on her own!' he exploded.

'No, no. There's a couple of our lot in there as well but

Bob's keeping them out of the way—' The man broke off when there was a shout from inside the cavern.

Alex didn't waste any more time debating the issue. He simply scooped up a helmet and ran into the tunnel. He could hear a commotion up ahead but it wasn't until he got to the bottom of Solomon's Chute that he discovered what had happened. His heart sank when one of the team tersely informed him that Fran and the girl they'd been trying to rescue were both in the pool and that they needed some more men to help to pull them out.

He quickly made his way along the passage and found Bob crouched on the ledge. He was attempting to throw a rope to Francesca but it was obvious that she wouldn't be able to catch it while she was keeping herself and the girl afloat. Kicking off his shoes, Alex jumped into the water and swam over to her.

'Give her to me and grab hold of that rope,' he instructed, his teeth chattering as the icy chill of the water seeped into his bones.

'Alex!' she exclaimed in amazement.

He took the limp form of the youngster from her and nodded towards the rope. 'Grab hold of that while Bob pulls you out,' he said, his teeth chattering.

Fortunately, she didn't argue and grabbed the rope, wrapping it around her arm and holding on while Bob hauled her up onto the ledge. As soon as she was out of the water, Bob tossed the line down to him and Alex fastened it around the girl. The current was tugging at his legs and he had to kick strongly to stop himself being carried away but it was easier once he no longer had to support the teenager.

Another couple of men had arrived by then and between them they managed to haul Sarah out of the water. Then it was his turn only his hands were so cold by that point that he couldn't get hold of the rope. In the end one of the rescue

team jumped in and tied the line around him so he could
be pulled out.

His limbs were numb with cold so walking back along
the tunnels wasn't easy but he forced himself to keep going
because he'd never hear the end of it if they had to carry
him out on a stretcher. Fran came rushing over when he
emerged from the cave, the relief on her face clear to see.

'Are you all right, Alex? You must be frozen…'

'I'm fine,' he said softly, his eyes saying everything he
couldn't with people watching. 'How about you?'

'I'm fine, too,' she replied, and his heart caught when he
read the answering message in her eyes.

There was no time to say anything else because there was
too much to do. Someone found him a blanket so he stripped
off his trousers and sweater and wrapped himself in it while
Fran attended to Sarah. The girl was very cold and shocked
but she seemed otherwise unhurt so they wrapped her in
some more blankets and handed her over to the paramedics
when the ambulance arrived.

There was a brief discussion about whether he should go
to the hospital as well but Alex declined the offer and that
was that…only it wasn't, was it? The rescue may have
ended successfully but there were all sorts of other issues
that still needed sorting out, the main one being what he
and Fran were going to do from here on in. Discovering
that she'd been in danger had made him see just how important she was to him and there was no way he could
ignore his feelings any longer. He loved her, very much,
too, but how did she feel about him?

That was the sixty-four-thousand-dollar question and he
knew he wouldn't be able to rest until he found out the
answer so it was little wonder that his cardiovascular system
got another good workout when she came across to him.
She'd changed back into her track suit and looked a lot more

presentable than he did, dressed in an old army-issue blanket, a fact she wasn't slow to remark on.

'I think you'd better change before you go to the surgery,' she said, smiling at him. 'Not that I'm casting aspersions on your dress sense, of course, but your current ensemble could prove less than inspiring for our patients.'

'Cheek! And after I did my Sir Galahad act by jumping in to save you.'

She chuckled. 'Oh, my hero!'

'I wish I was, Fran.'

He hadn't meant to say that and held his breath as he watched myriad expressions cross her face before she looked directly at him.

'You'll always be a hero in my eyes, Alex.'

He couldn't help himself then. There may have been a dozen reasons why he shouldn't have done what he did next but he could no longer remember a single one of them. Bending forward, he kissed her on the lips and it felt like a homecoming in every sense of the word.

'I'll get changed,' he said softly. 'On one condition.'

'And that is…?'

'That you promise you'll hurry through your list tonight. OK, so I know that isn't the kind of approach we dedicated GPs would normally apply to our work but I need to talk to you, Fran. I need to tell you things and hear what you have to say…' He tailed off because he didn't know how to explain the urgency he felt. He had a horrible feeling that if he didn't grab the opportunity while he had the chance, it might slip right through his fingers.

'And I want to talk to you, too, so I'll be extremely efficient. Whip 'em in and whip 'em out will be my motto tonight.'

He laughed at that, feeling some of his tension ease because it was silly to start imagining he'd had a premonition.

'It might not be that easy, I'm afraid. Everyone will want to hear all the gory details…'

'Then we'll get Mary to give them to them.'

Reaching up, she kissed him on the cheek—the lightest, briefest kiss imaginable—but it was such a huge step that he wanted to punch the air in triumph.

'I'll see you back at the house after surgery,' he murmured, his head reeling.

'First one back opens the wine.' She gave him a quick smile then hurried away and he didn't try to detain her because he knew that if he didn't let her go now then he might never be able to let her leave.

He took a deep breath as he went back to his car because that was the whole point, wasn't it? He wanted to be with her every minute of every day and it was mind-blowing to realise it, but was it really possible to make that wish come true? Even leaving aside the problem of Daniel's reaction to having another woman in his life, there was Fran to consider. How could he be sure that she was ready to move on?

Panic gripped him because he had to face the facts. She had been badly hurt and it wasn't as though she had resolved things with her fiancé because she'd not seen him since he'd fled the country. Although Alex hated the idea, how could he be sure she wasn't on the rebound? Her emotions were bound to be very mixed up after what she'd been through and he couldn't bear to think that he might be a substitute.

Could he honestly justify upsetting Daniel's life on that basis? he wondered, his heart aching as he was forced to confront the issue head on. It would be different if Fran loved him—he would move mountains to ensure they could be together. But did she? Could she? Would she?

He closed his eyes as the doubts hammered at him from all sides. He desperately wanted to believe there could be a happy ending for them but there was no guarantee.

* * *

Fran went straight to the surgery as soon as she got back to Teedale and did her best to speed things up but, as predicted, the patients refused to be hurried. Everyone she saw wanted to hear about what had gone on and congratulate her on her bravery. In the end, she had to grit her teeth and accept it but by the time the last unwilling bottom had been prised off its seat, she was fairly champing at the bit.

'I have to dash,' she told Mary, dropping the files into the tray as she rushed into the office. 'Would you mind filing these for me in the morning?'

'No, of course not. Oh, did you hear how that poor girl was…?'

Fran whisked out of the door, cutting off the receptionist in mid-flow.She would apologise tomorrow but there was no way she could stay there chatting when every fibre of her being was urging her to get back to the house and wait for Alex. He still had a couple of patients to see so it would give her time to make herself look presentable.

She smiled ruefully because she'd never envisaged herself thinking such a thing when she'd accepted this job. She'd wanted to hide away and lick her wounds because she'd been so badly hurt yet none of that seemed to matter now. Alex had shown her that she wasn't to blame for what had gone on. He'd set her free to love again.

She stopped dead because the thought was too enormous to deal with while she was walking. Was it possible that she'd fallen in love with him? It should have been the most ridiculous idea of all time but it wasn't. She only had to remember how she'd felt in the cave when she'd realised that she wanted to stay in Teedale so she could be with him, so it was the natural conclusion. It was a genuine, bona fide thought that needed considering and she wasn't sure if she could do that while she was with him.

She took a deep breath because she knew what would happen if she went back to the house. They would end up in bed together but was that what she wanted at the moment? Would it be right? Alex was the sort of man who wouldn't settle for less than total commitment but was she capable of giving him that after what Paul had put her through? The one thing she wouldn't do was hurt Alex by leading him on unless she was sure about what she wanted.

Fran turned around and made her way back along the street. The plumber had started work on the cottage and everywhere was in a mess but she had nowhere else to go. Taking the key out of her bag, she let herself in, trying to ignore the mound of pipes stacked in the middle of the sitting-room floor. Home sweet home it wasn't but it was a bolt-hole, a place where she could think about what she should do.

She went upstairs and lay down on the bed. She knew Alex would wonder where she'd got to but she needed time on her own before she saw him again. She couldn't afford to make a mistake because it wasn't just her life that would be ruined if she got this wrong but his as well.

Her heart ached because the thought of hurting him was too painful to bear. That was why she needed to be absolutely certain about what she wanted before she did anything.

Alex checked the kitchen clock for the umpteenth time, wondering where Fran had got to. He'd been back at home for almost an hour and there was still no sign of her. He went out to the hall and dialled the surgery on the off-chance that she might have forgotten something and gone back there, but after a couple of rings the answering-machine cut in.

He dropped the receiver back into its cradle and frowned because, logically, the only other place she could be was the cottage. He had no idea what she could be doing there when the place was in such a mess...

Unless she was avoiding him?

His breath caught painfully because he should have realised what had happened. She'd had second thoughts about tonight, probably second *and* third thoughts about him! Maybe she'd realised that she was getting in too deep and it wasn't what she wanted. He supposed he should be glad that she'd called a halt before the situation had progessed any further but for the life of him he couldn't find anything positive about it. He loved her and he didn't want to lose her before he'd had the chance to win her but he might not have a choice in the matter.

Fran had to decide what she wanted—and he couldn't make that decision for her.

Morning light spilled into the bedroom but Fran was already awake. She'd slept very little because her mind had been too busy to allow her to rest. Last night she'd done what she'd believed necessary—given herself the time and the space to think—but it hadn't achieved anything. She still didn't know what she was going to do about Alex.

She got up, grimacing when she saw the crumpled state of her clothes. There was no way she could turn up for work looking like this so she would have to go back to the house and get changed. She checked her watch as she made her way downstairs and was relieved to see that it was barely five o'clock. Alex would still be in bed at this hour of the morning so she could slip into the house without him noticing. She would have to speak to him at some point, of course, but the longer she could put it off, the more chance she had of making up her mind. She had to be certain that she could give him what he needed and not risk breaking his heart.

The house was silent when she let herself in a short time later and she breathed a sigh of relief as she crept upstairs to her room. She took a shower then put on her dressing-

gown and just as quietly made her way down to the kitchen.
A cup of tea should help to settle her nerves before she
confronted Alex. She only hoped he wasn't angry with her
for cutting and running—

She stopped dead when she opened the kitchen door and
saw him sitting at the table. He obviously hadn't been to
bed because he was still wearing the same clothes he'd had
on the night before and her heart ached because it didn't
take a genius to work out why he'd been sitting there all
night.

'Another early bird,' he said in a voice that sounded gritty
with tiredness. 'Couldn't you sleep?'

'No. I…I was too tired to relax.' She glanced around,
wondering if it might be wiser to make her escape while
she had the chance, but he forestalled her.

'Sit yourself down and I'll make you a cup of tea.' He
didn't wait for her to answer as he got up and switched on
the kettle. 'Milk no sugar, isn't it?' he asked over his shoulder.

'Yes.' She dredged up a smile although she didn't know
how she was going to sit there, drinking tea, as though nothing had happened. 'You must have a good memory if you
can remember details like that.'

'It's not that difficult to remember the likes and dislikes
of the people you care for.'

Her heart caught and she looked blindly at him through
a mist of tears. 'I'm so sorry, Alex.'

'Why should you be sorry because you acted sensibly?'
He shrugged, his broad shoulders lifting tiredly beneath the
crumpled white shirt. 'I'm grateful that one of us had the
sense not to rush into a situation we would have ended up
regretting.'

'Would we? You're sure it would have been the wrong
thing to do?' she asked, needing him to tell her that she'd
made the right decision. Maybe she couldn't put her hand

on her heart and swear that sleeping with him would have been the right thing to have done but neither could she swear that it would have been wrong. The realisation made her feel more confused than ever.

'As sure as I can be about anything these days,' he said with a wry little smile that twisted her heartstrings.

'I just thought…' She stopped and bit her lip, not even certain if it would be right to explain how confused she felt.

'You thought what?' he prompted as he came back to the table. He sat down and took her hand, his fingers closing gently around hers. 'Tell me what you were going to say, Francesca.'

'I just thought it would be better not to rush things,' she said slowly, trying to quell the shiver that danced down her spine when she felt the warm strength of his hand encircling hers. 'I needed time to think about what was happening.'

'Very sensible,' he said deeply, his thumb absently caressing the back of her hand.

Fran drew her hand away and tucked it in her lap because she knew how dangerous it was to allow the contact to continue. She was far too aware of him without making the situation any more fraught. For either of them.

Her breath caught when she looked at him and saw the tenderness in his eyes as well as the need. She couldn't remember anyone looking at her this way before and it was incredibly moving to witness it now. There was no doubt in her mind that Alex wanted her in every way a man could want a woman but his desire was tempered by tenderness and concern and it was difficult not to let that affect her.

'I don't want to do anything that might…hurt you,' she said huskily, wondering how best to explain. 'Past experiences have left me feeling very bruised and I'm not sure if I can give you what you want, Alex.'

An expression of pain crossed his face and he looked down at the table for a moment before he met her gaze.

'And I don't want to push you into something which you might ultimately regret. I know you've been through a lot, Fran. You were let down by someone you loved and you need time to recover from that. It would be silly to make any more mistakes.'

'Y-e-s…' she said slowly because she wasn't sure if he'd really understood what she'd been trying to tell him, that she was afraid she might not be capable of the kind of commitment he deserved.

'That's why you were right not to come back to the house last night because we both know what would have happened.'

'And it wasn't what you wanted either?' she asked when she caught the undercurrent in his voice.

'I'm not sure.' He shrugged when she looked at him in surprise. 'I wanted to make love to you, Fran, and I won't deny that. But I wasn't sure if it was the right thing to do.'

'So you're glad I stayed away?' she prompted, somewhat hurt by the admission.

'"Glad" probably isn't the word I'd use,' he said with a touch of asperity that made her smile.

'Relieved then?'

'I suppose so. I wouldn't do anything to hurt you, Fran. You've been through enough.'

He brushed his knuckles down her cheek in the gentlest of caresses imaginable yet she felt a spasm of raw need sear through her the moment his skin made contact with hers. She sat stock-still, not even daring to breathe in case it unleashed all the emotions that seemed to be swirling around them at that moment. She heard Alex suck in a ragged breath and the sound of it being drawn into his lungs seemed to reverberate inside her until every pulse was suddenly beating to the same tempo.

'Francesca.'

His voice ached with hunger as he whispered her name

and she shuddered. There was a moment when they both stared at one another, transfixed, before he suddenly leant across the table and kissed her.

Fran gave a small murmur almost of relief as she bent forward and kissed him back. Maybe she hadn't decided what she was going to do but it no longer seemed to matter. The only important thing at that moment was this need she felt to let him know how much she cared for him. And she did.

He uttered something harsh as he tore his mouth away from hers and stood up. Fran stumbled to her feet as he came around the table. She was already reaching for him when he took her in his arms. He kissed her with a passion that made the blood scorch her veins and she gasped. Heat poured through her as she wound her arms around his neck and drew his head down so she could deepen the kiss, her tongue sliding between his lips and mating with his. She heard him groan deep in his throat and the sound made her whole body throb with desire. It was blatantly obvious how aroused he was when he pressed her against him but she wasn't shocked by it. Why should she be? Alex wanted her and she wanted him, too. Just as much.

He dragged his mouth away and she could hear the struggle he was having to retain control in the roughened timbre of his voice. 'If this isn't what you want, Francesca, then say so because I don't think I'll be able to stop if we go any further.'

'But I don't want you to stop,' she murmured, nibbling his jaw.

'Are you sure?' He gripped her by the shoulders and set her away from him so that he could look into her eyes. 'This is a big step and I'll understand—'

She didn't let him finish, didn't want to hear any more because her body was clamouring with need and for the moment that was all that mattered. She wanted to make love with him while the world and all their problems faded away.

She kissed him on the mouth and her lips were every bit as insistent as his had been as she drew the response she wanted from him. When he swept her up into his arms and carried her along the hall there was triumph mingled with her pleasure. Morning sunlight was dappling the room when he laid her on his bed and she smiled, thinking how right it was that they should have sunshine after the darkness they'd both endured.

He slowly untied the belt of her robe and smiled wickedly at her. 'This is even better than opening a Christmas present.'

Fran laughed, loving the fact that even in the throes of passion he could tease her. 'How can you be sure?'

'Because I know that I'm going to love what's inside this wrapper,' he murmured, parting her robe and gazing at her in a way that made a flush of heat touch her skin. He kissed her gently on the lips then closed the robe over her nakedness again and smiled into her eyes.

'If I don't cover you up I'll never be able to undo all these fiddly little buttons on my shirt.'

'Don't worry. I'll do them for you.'

She sat up and started to unbutton his shirt, feeling the tremor that ran through her body as inch after inch of delectable flesh appeared. Alex's skin was lightly tanned, his muscles firm and well developed, the cushiony pad of hair in the centre of his chest tickling her knuckles as she worked the buttons free, and she fumbled as a wave of longing washed over her.

'Having trouble?' he asked, the jaunty note in his voice at odds with the tremor that was working its way through the powerful muscles beneath her hands.

'No, just taking my time,' she replied sweetly, letting her

fingers trail tantalisingly along his breastbone for the sheer pleasure of feeling him quiver with longing.

He laughed throatily as he bent and nibbled her ear while she undid the rest of the buttons so that it took her far longer than it should have done. He sat back and grinned at her when the last button finally slid out of its buttonhole. 'Took your time, didn't you?'

'I was somewhat hampered,' she retorted haughtily then gasped when he extracted a very effective punishment for speaking to him in that tone.

Fran sank back against the pillows, her eyes half-closed as he continued to kiss her—long, drugging kisses that made her feel boneless and as though she was melting. He drew back and dragged off his shirt, tossed it aside then bent over her again and took hold of the edges of her robe.

'A pleasure postponed,' he whispered, his breath warm on her skin as he parted the fabric so that she was revealed to his gaze.

Fran gasped when his eyes skimmed over her. Even though he was only looking and not touching, she could feel desire burning inside her. When he laid his hand flat on her breast she cried out and heard him groan when her nipple pressed itself shamelessly into his palm.

He caressed her with infinite care and unbearable tenderness, his fingers tracing the contours of her breasts as though he was mentally mapping their shape and feel. Then when she thought that the level of pleasure she was experiencing couldn't be surpassed, he suckled her and she cried out when she felt him draw her nipples into his mouth. Needles of pleasure were shooting through her, building with each second that passed until she was sure that she couldn't stand any more, yet there was much more to come.

Alex swiftly shed the rest of his clothes and lay down beside her and she shivered in delight when she felt the long, hard muscles in his thighs against her own. She reached for him, not trying to disguise her eagerness as she caressed him, and he shuddered then gently removed her hand, placing a kiss in the centre of her palm before he laid it by her side.

'My turn now,' he whispered, his eyes smiling at her in a way that filled her with heat. He kissed her on the mouth, another long, drugging kiss that made her feel as though she was floating in a sea of pleasure. When his mouth slid to her jaw then to her neck and her breasts, she murmured in delight. Everywhere his lips touched, she felt nerves tingling, exploding.

His mouth travelled lower, skimming over her midriff, her stomach, the curve of a hip, the firmness of a thigh and still her pleasure grew. He paused at her left knee, gently nibbling the soft skin on the inside and successfully wringing a moan from her before he moved to her calf and then her ankle. Another pause there made her shift restlessly because the desire that was building inside her was fast reaching a peak, but he refused to be hurried even when she tried to encourage him by murmuring his name in a voice that echoed with passion.

He lavished attention on her ankle bone then moved to her instep and she knew that she couldn't let him continue when every fresh caress was in danger of driving her over the edge. She sat up and grasped his shoulders, feeling goose-bumps break out on his skin the moment she touched him. It was such an elemental response that it stunned her for a moment, but he straightened up and as soon as she saw the desire in his eyes, every other thought except one fled.

'Make love to me,' she demanded because there was no point being coy when it was what they both wanted so desperately.

He didn't say a word, didn't need to as he eased her back against the pillows and kissed her with heart-rending tenderness. Fran closed her eyes as she gave herself to him, letting her body glory in what was happening as they reached undreamed of heights together. It was everything that love-making should be and so different to what she'd experienced with Paul that she realised how foolish she'd been to imagine that she'd loved him.

This was what love felt like, this joining of the spirit as well as the body. If she'd had any doubts, she didn't have them any longer. She loved Alex not just because he'd set her free but because of who he was. He was the man she wanted to spend her life with and soon—very soon—she would tell him that...

CHAPTER TWELVE

THE early morning sunshine had soon turned to rain. Alex lay in bed and watched the raindrops running down the window. His body felt totally relaxed and at ease yet his mind was once again in turmoil.

He rolled onto his side, taking care not to wake Francesca who had fallen asleep beside him. Making love with her had been every bit as wonderful as he'd imagined it would be and that's what worried him. Now that he'd tasted such pleasure it was going to be harder than ever to behave sensibly. He knew she'd been deeply moved by the experience...he had to pause at this point because the thought needed to be savoured...but he mustn't read too much into her response. She'd been through a lot and making love with him might have been the release she'd needed rather than the commitment he yearned for.

Her eyes suddenly opened and he saw her pupils dilate when she saw him. Panic gripped him because he didn't think he could bear it if she was upset because of what they'd done.

'Good morning,' he said hurriedly, wanting to speak first and thereby set the tone. Nothing too heavy, he decided. Nothing that would scare her or make her think that he expected anything from her...

'And good morning to you, too.' A brilliant smile lit her face as she leant forward and kissed him on the mouth. 'For the second time!'

Alex let out a whoop of relief. The fact that she didn't seem to have any regrets made him feel ten times better. 'Well, I for one have to say that the second time is the best.'

'And I'd have to agree with you.'

She kissed him again, with tenderness not the passion he would have preferred, but he could put up with that, he assured himself. His body suddenly sprang into action again, making a mockery of that fine sentiment, and he groaned when she chuckled.

'Ignore it. I'll take a cold shower or something.'

'If that's what you prefer...although I do know another way.'

She smiled into his eyes as she slid her hand beneath the covers and began to stroke him intimately. Alex gasped because his response although predictable was rather alarming. He'd had four years of celibacy and, apart from the odd twinge, he'd coped extremely well. But there was little doubt that if he didn't make love to her again soon, he might just explode!

Their coupling was fast and furious this time, a frenzy that stemmed from need and passion yet which contained so much more than either of those emotions that it brought tears to his eyes. Alex buried his face in her throat, unsure how she would react if she realised how moved he was. She might be happy to enjoy a passionate fling with him but there was nothing to say that she was prepared to have any strings attached to it.

'Alex?'

Her voice echoed with concern and he sighed guiltily because he was such a lousy actor, it was little wonder he'd been rumbled.

'I know. And I'm sorry, too.'

'Sorry? Because what we did meant something to you?'

She gently tugged on his hair so that he was forced to look at her and the warmth in her eyes made his fears seem foolish but he had to be sure that he made his position perfectly clear.

'Mmm. I don't want to put you in a difficult position,

Fran. I know that getting involved with me wasn't on your agenda.'

He had to pause at that point because the thought of losing her was too much to contend with and she quickly stepped into the silence.

'But that doesn't mean we can't feel real emotions, Alex. It doesn't mean that you have to be sorry because you care.' She cupped his cheek and his heart ached when he saw the tears that were trembling on her lashes now. 'I like it that you care. It feels wonderful to know that I'm not just anyone to you.'

'You could never be that,' he told her simply and with unashamed honesty because it was important they got this straight at least. 'When I hold you in my arms, you couldn't be anyone but you. You're too beautiful and too special.'

'Thank you.'

She kissed him softly on the mouth and he sighed when he tasted the salt from her tears mingling with the sweetness of her lips. He knew they had skated over the issue of what they both wanted and that the problem wasn't going to go away. It was a relief in a cowardly way when he heard Daniel going downstairs because it meant he could avoid the subject for a while longer.

'I'd better get downstairs before Daniel wreaks havoc in the kitchen,' he said, dropping a last kiss onto her mouth as he tossed back the quilt.

'And I'd better get back to my own room.' She treated him to a conspiratorial smile as she reached for her robe. 'We don't want an inquisitive eight-year-old finding us both in here, do we?'

'Not if we want to avoid the million and one questions that would surely follow,' he agreed, wondering why he felt so deflated when she was being so understanding. It went without saying that he didn't want Daniel finding out about them until he knew how it was going to affect him so it was ridiculous to feel so disheartened. Was it the fact that he sensed she was as eager as he was to avoid a discussion?

It was difficult to deal with the thought after she left. As he went into the bathroom, he reminded himself of the reason why they mustn't rush things: naturally, Francesca would have doubts about getting involved in another relationship and he had Daniel to consider. However, he would have felt so much better if he'd had an idea how she really felt about what they'd done. Had it been a *never-to-be-repeated* experience they should both try to forget, or had it been the start of something more?

He sighed because he would just have to be patient a while longer.

Francesca was at her desk way before the time she needed to be there but she'd felt the need to get out of the house. Making love with Alex had been everything she could have wished for but it hadn't solved her main problem about what she should tell him.

She loved him yet she couldn't quite bring herself to tell him that. Although there was no doubt in her mind that he'd been affected by their love-making, she wasn't sure if it had meant as much to him as it had to her. Maybe it was that comment he'd made about feeling guilty that had awoken these doubts but until she was sure of his feelings, she didn't intend to put him under any pressure. Telling him that she wanted to spend her life with him might not be what he wanted to hear.

It was a depressing thought, even more so after the euphoria that she'd experienced earlier in the day, and she found it difficult to put on a brave face. Once again a lot of the patients she saw were eager to hear about her experiences in the cavern and it was hard to respond positively when the incident had been superseded by other events.

She worked her way through her list then took an early

lunch because there was an anti-smoking clinic that afternoon. Alex was rostered for house calls that day so he'd left by the time she went back to work. There were half a dozen people in the waiting room so she took them into Alex's consulting room because it was the largest and they were doing group therapy work. Hilary was helping out as usual and she handed round the notes that Fran had printed out for everyone to read.

'Welcome to the anti-smoking clinic,' she said once everyone was comfortably settled. 'I know a few of you will have tried to give up smoking before and failed but this time you are going to beat the habit.'

'Mind over matter, eh?' Alan Hanley, the local odd-job man, quipped.

'In a way, yes, it is. You have to be fully committed to the idea of stopping smoking or you'll never succeed.' She held up the fact sheet she'd prepared for them. 'Hopefully, this will convince you why it's so important. Over one hundred thousand deaths a year can be attributed to tobacco smoking. It causes lung cancer, mouth and throat cancer, bronchitis and emphysema as well as cardiovascular diseases. If that isn't enough to put you off, it also causes your teeth to turn yellow and your skin to age.'

She looked round and smiled. 'Am I trying to scare you? Yes, I am. I enjoy my job but I'm not so desperate for patients that I won't try to discourage you from doing long-term damage to yourselves. Smoking kills and the sooner you accept that, the sooner you will want to stop doing it.'

She'd obviously shocked them by her no-nonsense approach but she knew how important it was to set the tone from the beginning. Once everyone had recovered from their surprise, they began asking questions and she was pleased to hear how positive they all sounded. By the time the session ended, she was fairly sure that most of the people present that day would come back the following week. Hilary helped her tidy away the chairs and they were just stacking the last one in the storeroom when someone knocked on the outer doors.

'I'll go,' Hilary offered. 'It's probably the courier from the chemist's wanting to collect the prescriptions.'

'Thanks. I'll just write up my notes then call it a day,' Fran agreed, heading into her room. She sat down at her desk and jotted down the names of everyone who'd attended the clinic then glanced up when Hilary appeared.

'Sorry, Fran, it wasn't the chemist but someone to see you.'

'It's a bit early for evening surgery,' she said, glancing at the clock.

'It isn't a patient. He says he's a friend of yours. Paul Bryant. Shall I send him in?'

'Paul!' Fran couldn't hide her shock as she rose to her feet.

'Yes.' Hilary looked at her in concern. 'I'll send him packing if you don't want to see him.'

'No, it's all right.' She took a deep breath because there was no way she was going to let Paul think she was afraid to speak to him. She had no idea what he wanted or how he came to be here but she wasn't going to run away and hide again because of him.

The thought stiffened her spine and she stood up straighter. 'I'll see him, Hilary. Can you send him through, please?'

'If you're sure.' Hilary still looked troubled as she hurried away.

Fran went over to the window and stared out at the now-familiar view. She'd been in Teedale just a short time yet she'd grown to love this village and felt at home here, more at home than she'd ever felt in London. Her reasons for moving here may have been painful but she realised with a flash of insight that the result had more than made up for it.

She'd come here and met Alex and it had been a turning point in her life because she'd found what had been lacking before. Nothing Paul said or did could alter that fact; nothing he said or did could affect her. He was part of her past and he had nothing to do with her future.

'Hello, Fran. Surprised to see me?'

She glanced round when she recognised his voice and took stock of the man who once she'd believed had held her happiness in the palms of his hands. Paul was extremely good-looking in an urbane kind of way but her tastes had changed. She preferred a man with character now and Paul's face lacked character because he lacked it himself.

'I can see you are.' He smiled as he came into the room, his lips curling in a way that once upon a time had made her legs tremble. Now it didn't mean a thing. 'I probably should have phoned first—'

'What do you want?' she asked sharply, cutting him off in mid-flow so that he blinked in surprise.

'I wanted to apologise for what happened, of course.' He treated her to another of those warmly intimate smiles, blissfully unaware that she was immune to them now. 'I know I behaved very badly and I'm truly sorry for what I did. But I was hoping we might be able to work something out.'

'And what precisely were you hoping to work out?'

'You, me, this mess we're in.' He shrugged as he glanced around the room. 'You must have thought it was a good idea to come here but you don't really want to be stuck in the back of beyond, do you? If we can sort out that little problem we had with the police, you could move back to London—'

'*I* didn't have a problem with the police, Paul. You did. You were the one who conned all that money out of those people. The fact that you also conned me out of a lot of money is immaterial but don't think I'm ready to forget what you did.'

'Oh, come on, Fran! It was just a blip, sweetheart. Surely you're not going to let a few thousand pounds come between us?'

He came over to the window and she stiffened when he turned her to face him. 'We were good together, babe, and we could be just as good again if you'd only give me another chance. I know what I did was wrong but I'm hoping you can find it in your heart to forgive me. I missed you *so* much, my sweet. That's why I came back to England. I just couldn't bear to be without you any longer!'

'You're right, Paul, because what you did was wrong,' she said coldly, ignoring that last comment because it wasn't worth sullying her lips by repudiating it. She stepped back, forcing him to release her. 'There is no *us*, Paul. There never was, actually. You just used me for your own ends and that's it as far as I'm concerned.'

'I understand why you feel like this,' he said softly, looking contrite. 'What I did was inexcusable. All I can say in my own defence is that I was under a lot of pressure at the time.'

'Pressure of your own making,' she pointed out. 'Nobody forced you to gamble away all that money the same as nobody forced you to steal from all those people who'd entrusted you with their savings.'

'I know, I know!' He ran his hands through his hair. 'I was a fool, Fran, and I admit it. I swear that I'll do everything I can to make amends but, please, *please*, don't turn your back on me. All I want is another chance—'

'I'm sorry but I am not prepared to discuss this any more.' She went back to her desk and sat down. 'Goodbye, Paul.'

'I'm not giving up,' he warned her, heading for the door. 'I'll win you round somehow even if I have to spend the next fifty years doing so!'

'Then all I can say is that you'll be wasting your time because I'm not interested.'

She picked up her notes, making it clear that the conversation was over, and after a moment, she heard the door closing as he left. She could only hope it was the last she saw of him because it had made her see what a fool she'd been to believe that she'd ever been in love with him.

Paul's apologies were so much hot air: they didn't really mean anything. She wasn't sure why he'd come but she didn't doubt that he had his own agenda. Maybe he thought he would have a better chance of receiving a light sentence when his case went to court if she was standing by him. That would be typical of Paul because his sole concern was himself and he cared nothing for anyone else's happiness.

Unlike Alex.

She gasped because all of a sudden it was as plain as the nose on her face: Alex had put her happiness first. He'd held back that morning and not told her how he'd felt because he'd been afraid that she hadn't wanted to hear it. Nobody could have made love to her the way he'd done and not felt deeply, and certainly Alex couldn't!

What an idiot he was, she thought, her heart overflowing with love. What an idiot she'd been, too, because she was just as guilty but she would soon rectify their mistakes. She would tell him how she felt and then make him tell her the truth about *his* feelings.

Alex was on his way back to the surgery after finishing the house calls when he realised that he'd forgotten to buy the stamps. Mary had asked him to get them to save her having to go to the post office and she would give him a real rollicking if he went back without them. He parked outside the post office and got out of the car. He was just about to open the door when Hilary came out so he paused to speak to her.

'How did the anti-smoking clinic go?'

'Really well. Fran didn't pull her punches but I think the firm approach was the best to take.'

'Good.' His heart gave an appreciative little shudder at the mention of Fran's name and he summoned a smile because it wasn't the time or the place to let his libido run riot again. 'Let's hope she can keep them on the straight and narrow. Alan Hanley's cholesterol level is starting to look like the national debt and it would help bring it down if he gave up cigarettes.'

He was about to go into the shop when Hilary stopped him. 'Actually, something happened after the clinic finished,' she said hesitantly. 'Fran had a visitor.'

There was something in her voice that made his skin prickle in alarm and he turned to look at her. 'A visitor?'

'Mmm. A man.' Hilary shrugged but he could tell how uncomfortable she was, discussing it.

'Obviously, you're worried, Hilary, so why don't you tell me what happened?'

'I don't know if there's anything to tell, though. This man turned up and asked to speak to Fran and when I told her who he was, well, she looked really upset.'

'Did you get his name?' he demanded although he had a horrible suspicion that he already knew who the visitor had been.

'Paul Bryant. It doesn't mean anything to me—how about you?'

'I've heard of him.' He managed to shrug but every muscle in his body seemed to be in spasm all of a sudden. 'He was a friend of Fran's.'

'Oh, that's all right, then!' Hilary gave a little sigh of relief. 'Silly of me to worry, wasn't it?'

She said goodbye but it was a few seconds before Alex could summon the energy to go and buy his stamps. The thought of what might have been happening at the surgery made him feel positively ill with worry. What if Fran had realised that she was still in love with that Bryant fellow? he wondered hollowly as he got back into the car. What was he going to do then? What *could* he do?

He drove back to the surgery and his heart felt like a lead weight just hanging in his chest. It wasn't beyond the realms of possibility that Fran might forgive the rat who'd deserted her. After all, if she loved Bryant—really loved him with every fibre of her being the way he, Alex, loved her—anything was possible. Didn't people say that love could overcome any obstacles so getting through a court case would be chicken feed!

Fran was in the office when he went into the surgery and she looked round when she heard his footsteps. Alex steeled himself not to betray any emotion when he saw the happiness in her eyes. There was only one reason, to his mind, why she was looking as though Christmas and her birthday had both come together, and it didn't do a lot for his own mood.

'How did it go?' she asked brightly, smiling at him.

'How did what go?' he countered, dropping the bundle of files he'd taken with him into the filing tray.

'The calls. Were there any problems?'

'None I couldn't handle.' He glanced round when Mary came into the room and handed her the stamps. 'Here you are.'

Mary thanked him and went to put them away so he took the opportunity to make his escape. Quite frankly, the office was too small for him, Fran and all that bubbling happiness to reside comfortably together.

Striding along the corridor, he let himself into his room and hung his coat on the back of the door then sat down at his desk, wondering what he was going to do. Fran and Bryant. Bryant and Fran. Whichever combination he chose, it made him feel ill.

'Are you all right?'

She'd followed him into his room and he gritted his teeth when he looked up and saw her standing there. A few short hours ago he'd held her in his arms, loved her with every bit of his mind as well as his body and it was impossible to deal with the thought that he might never be able to do it again.

Making love with her had been the first step towards a permanent commitment, he realised all of a sudden. He may have told himself at the time that he wouldn't push her for more than she could give him but he would have done his damnedest to make her his. Now Bryant had come back into her life and Bryant was the man who probably would spend the rest of his life with her, not him. The thought almost made him weep.

'I'm fine. Why shouldn't I be?' he shot back in near despair.

'No reason I can think of but you're acting very strangely,' she replied, her smile fading when she caught the bite in his voice that pain had put there.

Alex knew that if he was to survive with at least his dignity intact, he had to take drastic measures. Although he desperately wanted to ask her what had happened between her and Bryant, he wasn't sure if he was up to hearing the answer right then. Could he trust himself to stand firm if she told him that she was going back to the other man? No way!

'Maybe I find it a bit awkward being around you after this morning,' he said, his heart contracting when he saw her draw back as though he had slapped her.

'I see. I didn't realise it was going to be a problem for you.'

'It won't be so long as we both understand that it was a one-off.'

'Of course.'

She turned away and it was all he could do not to drop

to his knees and beg her forgiveness when he saw her mouth quiver but sometimes it was necessary to be cruel to be kind. He didn't want her to think that she owed him anything in return for a couple of hours of passion!

'I…I'd better get ready before my patients arrive,' she said in a choked little voice as she hurried to the door.

'Good idea,' he agreed, feeling sick to his stomach because it was unbearably painful to deliberately hurt her like this. He lifted one of the files off the pile on his desk, not looking up until he heard the door close. Tossing the file back into the tray, he got up and went to the window, feeling pain clawing at his insides like a rabid animal.

He would never forgive himself for speaking to her in that fashion but what else could he have done? Told her that he loved her, longed for her, wanted to spend the rest of his life making her happy? Made a complete and utter fool of himself by pouring out his heart when she wasn't interested in *him* but Paul Bryant!

He swore colourfully, his frustration reaching a point whereby it had to erupt somehow. He felt a little calmer afterwards, calmer but not happier because happiness was no longer within his grasp. If he couldn't have Fran then he didn't think he could ever be truly happy again.

It was a complete nightmare!

Fran did her best to carry on in the days that followed but the tension between her and Alex affected every single thing she did. The fact that Paul had ignored her refusal to go back to him was an added strain that she could have done without. Every day flowers arrived at the surgery from him, each expensive arrangement accompanied by a tender little note, begging her forgiveness, and a couple of times he phoned and asked to speak to her although Fran refused to take his calls.

Mary was positively agog with excitement and obviously

desperate to know what was going on, but Alex ignored what was happening and it hurt Fran to realise that he didn't even care that Paul was trying to win her back. Maybe he was relieved that he was off the hook—and that thought hurt even more, of course.

Fortunately, she was able to move back into the cottage at the end of the week so that helped and it was certainly better than having to sleep under the same roof as Alex. Sleeping with him had done so much harm that she didn't know how they were ever going to get back to normal. She did her best to maintain a calm front at work but being around Alex, and knowing that he didn't care, was just too hard to bear in the end. There was only one way out of the mess, although it took her a whole weekend to make the decision. She would have to leave Teedale and find another job, and the sooner she did it, the easier it would be for everyone.

Alex was in the staffroom when she arrived for work on Monday morning. Once again there was another huge arrangement of flowers waiting for her and it was the final straw. Snatching the card off the Cellophane wrapping, she marched into the office and phoned the florist's and told the assistant that no more flowers were to be delivered to her under any circumstances. Even Paul should get the message that he was wasting his time—and his money—after that!

She didn't wait to hear what the woman had to say, just put the phone back on its rest and marched back to the staffroom, trying to ignore the pain she felt when she saw how drawn Alex looked as he glanced round from making himself a cup of tea.

'I've decided to find myself another job,' she said without any preamble. 'It's obvious that what happened between us is causing a problem so it seems the only sensible thing to do.'

'I see. I take it that you'll be going back to London?'

'I'm not sure where I'll be moving to until I see what's on offer,' she said, frowning because she wasn't sure why he seemed so positive that she would return to the city.

'But London would be more convenient. You'd be able to pick up the pieces again there,' he said, tossing the teabag into the waste bin.

'There aren't any pieces to pick up,' she replied shortly because it seemed such an insensitive comment to have made.

'Oh, come on, Fran. Don't be so coy. I don't know why you're trying to pretend when we both know why you want to go back to London.' He put the teaspoon on the counter and turned to face her. Fran felt her heart flutter because his expression was so grim. 'You're making a huge mistake.'

'I'm sorry but I have no idea what you're talking about—'

He gave a sharp downward thrust of his hand that was laced with impatience. 'Going back to Bryant is a mistake. I know you don't want to hear this but I have to say it. He used you once and he'll use you again. His type always does.'

'You...you think I'm going back to Paul?' she stammered.

'Of course. I saw how happy you looked the other day after he'd been here. Hilary told me about his visit, not that she needed to because I could have told by looking at you that something had happened. You were positively glowing, in fact.' He cast a disparaging glance at the bouquet. 'Add in the flowers and phone calls and it isn't difficult to work out what's going on. But you're making a mistake, Francesca, if you think he's right for you—'

'Just stop right there!' She stormed across the room and stood toe to toe with him. 'For your information I wouldn't have Paul back if you gift-wrapped him. He's a complete and utter sleazeball!'

'Sleazeball?' he repeated as though he'd never heard the term before which was odd because he was the one who'd first used it.

'Yes! He came here the other day fully convinced that all he had to do was crook his little finger and I'd go running back to him like a puppy but I soon put him right on that score!'

She jabbed a finger into his chest, felt him retreat a pace, and jabbed again because if ever there was a man who needed jabbing it was him. 'I told him that I wouldn't go back to him if I was desperate!'

Another jab only this time he stood his ground. 'Is that right?' he said softly and in a tone that made her toes curl before she forced them to behave.

'Yes! Oh, he gave me the usual sob story about how he'd missed me and couldn't bear to be without me but it was just the normal pack of lies.' She shrugged. 'Maybe he actually believes what he's saying and that's why he's so good at conning people but there is no way I'm being taken in again. Knowing Paul, he probably thought it would look good in court if I was standing by him. There's nothing like having an adoring little woman keeping the home fires burning while you do porridge, is there? I'm sure the jury would have loved that idea.'

'Doing porridge, eh? I never realised you were so familiar with the terminology.'

His voice seemed deeper all of a sudden, seductively, sexily deep, too. However, the hint of amusement it held wasn't lost on her either.

'I watch television, Dr Clever-Clogs! I'm as *au fait* with the jargon as the next person.'

'Oh, I'm sure you are. I'm not doubting you for a moment,' he said silkily, sitting down on the edge of the table.

'Good, because I'm fed up to the back teeth with people—correction with *men*—assuming things about me.'

'Is that a fact? So what assumptions have I made?'

'Do you want the full list or just the edited highlights?'

'The highlights will do.' His right hand snaked around her waist but she was too annoyed to worry about what he was doing.

'You *assumed* that I was going back to Paul. Wrong! You also *assumed* that I was happy because I'd seen him.' She laughed. 'Wrong again! You also *assumed*—'

'I've got the message. I'm a real klutz when it comes to understanding you, Fran, aren't I?' He sighed as his left hand joined his right and forged a link behind her back. 'It makes me afraid to leap to any more assumptions but there's just one I can't resist. However, before I take the plunge, maybe I should test out the theory behind it first.'

'What theo—'

The rest of the question got swallowed up as his mouth suddenly settled on hers. Fran put her hands on his shoulders but the urge to push him away was growing weaker by the nanosecond. His lips were warm and wonderfully tempting, so seductive as they urged hers to respond that she really couldn't hold out for very long. One nanosecond or maybe it was two were all she managed before she gave in and kissed him back.

Alex drew back and she could feel the shudder that passed through him as their mouths broke apart. 'I needed that,' he muttered hoarsely. 'I've been going crazy these past few days thinking that you were back with Bryant.'

'Good,' she said crossly. It hadn't been much fun for her either.

He chuckled as he pulled her back and cradled her against his heart which—just for the record—was racing. 'I'm an idiot, I know, but I couldn't help it.'

He set her away from him again and looked into her eyes with a wealth of love in his and everything that had been such a mess a few minutes earlier now became almost perfect.

'I love you, Fran. I need you, I want you, and I can't bear the thought of you leaving so please say that you will reconsider your decision.'

'You love me?' she whispered and he nodded, his eyes serious as they held hers.

'Yes. With my heart and my soul and every bit of my being.'

Now it was perfect! Now everything was right in her world and couldn't be better, except...

'I love you too, you idiot! If I was looking happy after Paul's visit it was because I'd made up my mind to tell you how I felt.' She grimaced. 'I'd kind of put it off that morning because I wasn't sure if I could do the whole commitment thingumabob, but I knew I could the moment I realised I couldn't live without you.'

'Oh, darling! I wanted to tell you how I felt but I was afraid of scaring you. I also wondered if you might have been on the rebound,' he admitted, and she glared at him.

'I am not on the rebound. I know how I feel and I love you, warts and all!'

'Makes me wish I could grow a few warts just for the fun of it,' he growled then pulled her to him again and kissed her thoroughly.

Fran kissed him back, letting him know how much he meant to her which was the whole world. They might have stayed there a lot longer if Mary hadn't suddenly appeared and just as hurriedly disappeared again when she saw what was happening.

Alex sighed as he rubbed his nose against hers. 'It will be all round the village by lunchtime, you realise.'

'What will?' she murmured.

'That we're getting married.' He chuckled when she

stared at him. 'We are, aren't we? I haven't made another wrong assumption, I hope?'

'No...I mean, yes. Yes, I'll marry you if that's what you want.'

'It is.' He kissed her tenderly. 'I want you for my wife as well as my partner, Francesca. That way we can spend all our time together.'

'Sounds good to me.' She kissed him gently then looked at him. 'What about Daniel, though? How will he react, do you think? I don't want him to get upset.'

'Which is why we shall both tell him tonight when he comes home from school. I don't know how he will take the news,' he admitted honestly. 'But I do know that I can't live without you and that I won't have to because you love me and that makes all the difference.'

He kissed her softly, lovingly then smiled at her. 'I would never disrupt his life unless I was sure that this was what we both wanted and I am. Daniel is a happy, well-adjusted little boy so all I can do is hope for the best.'

'All *we* can do,' she corrected, smiling. 'It's plural now, not single.'

'All *we* can do is hope for the best,' he confirmed, his voice grating because her words had touched him so deeply. He put his arms around her again and hugged her close. 'I have a feeling it's going to work out, though.'

'I hope so,' she murmured just a moment before he kissed her again. 'I really hope so...'

Three months later...

'Now, don't forget, Daniel, you need to hold up my train as I go up the steps.'

Fran turned away from the mirror and smiled at the little boy, wondering if anyone had ever felt as happy as she did at that moment. It was her wedding day and the village church would be packed with guests waiting to witness her marriage to Alex.

'No problemo,' Daniel assured her, adopting the voice of his favourite movie hero.

'Good. You're going to be a really brilliant page-boy,' she assured him.

She turned back to the mirror and took a last look at her reflection, hoping that Alex would approve of her dress. Made from the softest cream silk overlaid with lace, it was an absolute joy. Mary's sister had made it for her and she knew that she couldn't have found a more beautiful dress in any of the designer shops in London. Her flowers were a bunch of hand-tied roses and cornflowers which Kathleen Price had picked from her garden and made into a posy for her. Kathleen had also made her a simple headdress of roses which was the perfect complement to the gorgeous gown.

Everyone had been delighted when they'd heard she was marrying Alex and she'd been touched by all the support she'd had as she'd prepared for the wedding. However, the best thing of all had been Daniel's reaction. Despite their fears, he'd been thrilled when he'd found out that they were getting married and it had set the seal on their happiness. After today they would be a real family and, quite frankly, Fran couldn't wait!

'OK, let's go,' she said, turning away from the mirror. Her parents had flown back from Barbados for the ceremony and her father was waiting downstairs to escort her to the church. Fran was pleased that they'd come but nothing would have spoiled her happiness that day.

She took her father's arm as they left the cottage, smiling when she saw that the road outside was full of people waiting to see her leave. The people of this village had taken her into their midst and she loved being part of their community.

It took them just a few minutes to walk to the lovely old

church with its moss-covered roof and grey stone walls. She heard the wedding march starting up as the organist announced her arrival and then they were inside.

Fran walked up the aisle towards Alex and it felt as though her heart was overflowing with happiness when he turned to watch her and she saw the love on his face. This man wanted her now and for all eternity and he would never let her down, never disappoint her.

He stepped out of the pew and took her hand, turned and laid his other hand on his son's head, and she knew then that she was the luckiest woman in the world. She didn't even need to hear him whisper 'I love you' because she knew how he felt, just as he knew how she felt, too. She smiled up at him as the vicar took his place at the altar and the congregation fell silent, waiting to hear them make their vows. She had made her choice and she would never regret it because she'd chosen the right man.

Narrated with the simplicity and unabashed honesty of a child's perspective, *Me & Emma* is a vivid portrayal of the heartbreaking loss of innocence, an indomitable spirit and incredible courage.

ISBN 0-7783-0084-6

In many ways, Carrie Parker is like any other eight-year-old—playing make-believe, dreading school, dreaming of faraway places. But even her naively hopeful mind can't shut out the terrible realities of home or help her to protect her younger sister, Emma. Carrie is determined to keep Emma safe from a life of neglect and abuse at the hands of their drunken stepfather, Richard—abuse their momma can't seem to see, let alone stop.

On sale 15th July 2005

4 FREE

BOOKS AND A SURPRISE GIFT!

We would like to take this opportunity to thank you for reading this Mills & Boon® book by offering you the chance to take FOUR more specially selected titles from the Medical Romance™ series absolutely FREE! We're also making this offer to introduce you to the benefits of the Reader Service™—

> ★ FREE home delivery
> ★ FREE gifts and competitions
> ★ FREE monthly Newsletter
> ★ Exclusive Reader Service offers
> ★ Books available before they're in the shops

Accepting these FREE books and gift places you under no obligation to buy, you may cancel at any time, even after receiving your free shipment. Simply complete your details below and return the entire page to the address below. You don't even need a stamp!

YES! Please send me 4 free Medical Romance books and a surprise gift. I understand that unless you hear from me, I will receive 6 superb new titles every month for just £2.75 each, postage and packing free. I am under no obligation to purchase any books and may cancel my subscription at any time. The free books and gift will be mine to keep in any case.

M5ZED

Ms/Mrs/Miss/Mr ....Initials ....

BLOCK CAPITALS PLEASE

Surname ....

Address ....

....

....Postcode..

Send this whole page to:
UK: FREEPOST CN81, Croydon, CR9 3WZ